WAR CRIMES FOR THE HOME

WAR CRIMES
FOR THE HOME

LIZ JENSEN

BLOOMSBURY

First published 2002
Copyright © 2002 by Liz Jensen

Grateful acknowledgement is made to the following for permission to reprint
extracts from previously published material:

'Blue Skies Across Are Round the Corner'
Words and Music by Ross Parker and Hughie Charles
© Copyright 1937 Dash Music Limited, 8/9 Frith St, London W1.
Used by permission of Music Sales Ltd.
All Rights Reserved. International Copyright Secured.

'Smoke, Smoke, Smoke (That Cigarette)'
Words and Music by Merle Travis and Tex Williams
© 1947 by American Music Incorporated, USA.
Campbell Connelly and Company Limited,
8/9 Frith St, London W1.
Used by permission of Music Sales Ltd.
All Rights Reserved. International Copyright Secured.

'That Lovely Weekend'
Words by Moira Heath
Music by Ted Heath
© 1941 Chappell Music Ltd, London W6 8BS.
Reproduced by permission of International Music Publications Ltd.
All Rights Reserved.

The moral right of the author has been asserted

Bloomsbury Publishing Plc, 38 Soho Square,
London WID 3HB

A CIP catalogue record for this book
is available from the British Library

ISBN 0 7475 4747 5

10 9 8 7 6 5 4 3 2 1

Typeset by Palimpsest Book Production Limited,
Polmont, Stirlingshire
Printed and bound in Great Britain by
Clays Ltd, St Ives plc, Bungay, Suffolk

For my mother, Valerie Jensen, and in memory of my father, Niels Rosenvinge Jensen

'If you dig deep enough, all our secrets are the same'
– Amos Oz

JOKE

Here's a good one, Hank told it me.

Man goes to the doctor, and the doctor says, I have two pieces of very bad news for you.

OK, fire away, says the man.

Well, says the doctor. The first piece of very bad news is you have cancer. You are one hundred per cent riddled with it and you're going to die.

Oh, says the man. So what's the second piece of bad news then?

Well, says the doctor. It's this. You're also in the final stages of Alzheimer's disease. Your memory is full of holes.

Man thinks about that for a minute. And then he turns to the doctor.

Oh well, he says, best look on the bright side. At least I haven't got cancer!

That's a good joke, that is. But you know Hank's Wife? She didn't even laugh when Hank told it me. All she said was, What's got into you, Hank? What d'you want to go telling your poor old mum a tasteless joke like that for? You sick or what?

But me and Hank, we thought it was bloody funny. We laughed and laughed.

Here's another joke. There's this innocent lady seventy-nine and three-quarters, hasn't done nothing wrong, gets locked up in an old folks' home called Sea View cos she's losing her marbles.

But there ain't no humorous punchline, I'm afraid.

I FELL IN LOVE

I fell in love the same day a girl at the factory lost a quarter of herself.

Quite a day for maiming, quite a day for surprises. A dark winter morning, no lighting on the streets what with the blackout. Before you even reach the gates the sulphur crawls into your lungs, drainy and gaggy. In the locker room we call The Slops we wind on our cotton turbans. Different colour according to the shift you do, and I'm blue today, because I'm on the six-till-six, hair right up inside. Mr Simpson says the turbans is washed once a week but them nits aren't half breeders and there's no itching like nits under a turban. The Lousy Nitwits, we are.

—Mum would never've stood for this, I say to my sis Marjorie when we swap shifts. —Can you imagine what she'd say to Hitler?

—She'd say, Is it true you've only got one ball, mister? goes Marje.

Which is rubbish, because Mum was quality, she didn't have no dirty mouth, but it makes us laugh. Marje has Mum's mouth – the shape of it I mean, not the nicely-spokenness. But today she looks all in, in her orange turban. I'm prettier than Marje, and I notice it then. I even think: if it was marks out of ten she would be a six and I would be an eight-and-a-half. With lipstick

and powder, nine, I am not boasting I am just telling the truth here.

Before Mum's illness and 'To Be a Pilgrim' at the funeral, there was ironed sheets, proper scones, polished doorknockers, all the fusspot stuff that me and Marje used to laugh at which was also sneering. But with the war coming so soon after that, things got buggered and stayed that way, me and Marje not having any of Mum's famous elbow grease or whatever it was stopped mould growing indoors and butter going off. Just me and Marje in charge – just two stupid girls – and Dad posted off to Singapore to fight the Enemy, and then his letters that stopped coming. Sheets rumpled as they come, hens turning up in the kitchen to peck and splatter and Marje no longer a virgin because of Bobby.

Mum would've died.

Anyway Marje was lucky not to be on the day-shift as it turns out, wearing an orange turban and not a blue one like me and Iris. Lucky to be leaving to go home, so that all she heard was a faraway noise, and even then, she said, she never made the connection. She was tired, reckoned it was just a bomb, paid no notice. And when I mentioned it in Chicago later, she'd clean forgotten it. Funny the things you wipe out.

But I remembered. I was there.

There's a whole row of us working in blue turbans. Maisie Wheeler on one side of me, and Iris Jones on the other, and Maisie's yakking about a blast in Sheffield, hit a tram and got the driver and the conductress electrocuted.

—It shrank them both to the size of dolls! says Maisie. —I swear.

—Load of bollocks, says Iris, how can an electric current do that?

And I'm puzzling it over, it sounds true to me, because no one understands electricity, it is that close to magic,

4

and then the ten o'clock bell goes which is our cue for a sing-song so we forget about tram conductors shrunk to the size of dolls and away we go.

Along the street she wheels a perambulator,
She wheels it in the springtime and in the month of May,
And if you ask her why the hell she wheels it,
She wheels it for a soldier who is far, far away.
Far away, far away, far away, far away.
She wheels it for a soldier who is far, far away.

Iris is singing too. I know, because I'm standing right next to her. But my turning-blade has some muck in it, and all of a sudden I need a better rag, so I go up the line to get one from Mr Simpson, still singing.

Above the shelf her father keeps a shotgun,
He keeps it in the springtime and in the month of May,
And if you ask him why the hell he keeps it,
He keeps it for a soldier who is far, far away,
Far away, far away –

I've got my rag, and I'm just coming back. My mouth's still open from singing the chorus when it happens.

The bang's so loud it splits your head in half.

Then a big whoosh, and the whole world gets sucked up and thrown. And there's Iris, being chucked into the air like a little scrap. Torn apart, she is, because out gushes the red blood and there's bits that looks like meat from the butcher's. Maybe mince.

And you see her whole arm and shoulder spat sideways and flop to the floor. And there, look. There's her arm and her hand that has a ring on its finger which is not allowed in here because it says clearly in the rules, *No jewellery permitted*.

An engagement ring, it looks like. There's another surprise, see. She's a dark horse, ain't she?

I try to shut my mouth which is still open from the singing, but I can't. It's gone dry.

I just stare at Iris's arm and hand and shoulder on the floor, not wanting to look at the mince bit that's left behind possibly still alive cos it's screaming.

Damage: Total loss of one arm and one shoulder, because like Mr Simpson says, the manufacture of munitions is not a blinking joke, girls.

Talking of jokes, here is one. There's an optimist and a pessimist. The pessimist puts his head in his hands and moans, Oh God, things just can't get any worse! And you know what the optimist says, with a big smile on his face? He says, Oh yes they can!

Jokes cheers me up, so does food. No one knows how I can put away so much food, being so bloody old and with only half a duodenum, but I do. I am making up for when I was hungry. It's like there's this black hole inside me, won't never get filled no matter how much I shovel in.

SEA VIEW

In hospital after my duodenum, there was a window. Look out, and all you saw was a demolition site. They were pulling down a row of shops called The Parade, with a newsagent's and a dry cleaner's and Woolworth's. They emptied all the rubbish out in skips – furniture, metal desks and old strip-lights and uprooted carpeting. Then one morning – it must've crept in during the night – this big orange crane was on the site, planted behind Woolworth's like an iron tree. And the wrecking started. The crane, it had a wrecker ball. From where I was, I could watch it, this wrecker ball. It swung and it swung, knocking down roofs and brick walls, chucking out clouds of plaster and brickdust, and the walls tumbling sudden but slow, like butter melting in the microwave. Wrecking and wrecking. Watching it made you feel wild and a bit wuzzy, but you couldn't stop, your eyes stayed glued to it. Whole hours went by when all I did was watch it. I missed the bombs in the war. We heard violence all the time, the Moaning Minnies wailing, the Germans overhead, the sound of doodlebugs. Marje always said it was like the sound of silk being ripped. But we didn't see what they did till after the raid.

Then one morning I look out and the orange crane's gone, and the site's just a big empty space, just puddles and mud, and I've forgotten how it all looked before. I must've missed something. Missed the doodlebug, maybe the whole war, slept through it or been otherwise out to lunch. Because there was suddenly nothing. No crane, no nothing. No nothing left to wreck.

The wrecking was over.

And then the doctor told me I wasn't going back to Hank's place. It wasn't just my duodenum, see. It was a small stroke. A nice home called Sea View was waiting for me, and as soon as I was back to rights I could go out into the world again.

What world is this he's talking about, I thought. Do I know it?

I mean, is there jokes there? Is there decent food?

One thing I'll say is, it's a proper TV here, a big one with good strong colours that don't meddle with each other. That Marty Lone was on again, you remember him, he confessed he was a gay homosexual. He was saying he and his mother have a very close relationship, they're best friends, hers is the only tuna bake he'll eat. His lips look like they're made of rubber, the inside of a hot-water bottle if you've ever seen one slashed.

Cauliflower cheese for lunch. Mine had specks in it, I hate specks and I don't care who knows it, reminds me of the National Loaf in the war. When Ron first tasted it he spat it out, he said, You call that bread, man? Jeez, tastes like something died. Boy, are you a bunch of suckers.

—It's pepper, a half-dead old drooler called Doris piped up. —Stop making such a song and dance.

—I like to add my seasoning and condiments myself, as it happens, I told her. —Why's everyone so blinking old in here?

That corner of blue over there, that's the View part. You

can see the ferry going past, you can smell the cooking from it because holidays make you hungry and they'd best get a good meal down them before they go abroad which is where Hank used to go by HGV long-haul. He was doing the lorries then, red lorry yellow lorry I used to say to him, a tongue-twister when he was little. Must've had an influence.

—Hank's Wife hasn't seen fit to visit, I tell Doris.
—Better things to do with her time. She's got a lover. He's got one of them red cars with eyelids, comes and gives it her every Thursday.

—A change is as good as a rest, says Doris, letting her eye shut down like a little sash window.

—And that baby Calum's out of my hair too, I tell her. —They should get rid of that fake nipple of his, it's infested with germs. Just me and Hank.

—Hank?

—My son. American connections. Chicago. The windy city. I always said to Hank, if you shut your eyes, you'll remember it. Skyscrapers and blueberry muffins and all that. I call him Hank from those days, it's what his dad would've called him, it's what Americans call children.

—How long did you live there? she goes.

—What, Bristol?

—America.

—Never been there.

—What?

—Seen it on TV, Chicago and that. I had a GI boyfriend once. He fought in Tunisia and then he bombed Germany. Had a big scar on his thigh from shrapnel.

Doris looks at me.

—One Yank, she says. —Remember that? One Yank and they're off.

*　　*　　*

9

It's that night, the same day Iris gets blown up, that I begin to learn more about maiming. But it's not munitions this time. It's love.

I was never the brightest. But I wasn't stupid neither. I was middling.

—I hope he's not too clever for you, says Marjorie helping me get ready, going pish pish at my neck with the phoney black-market Chanel that don't even begin to smell like the real McCoy but it's better than nothing, ain't it. She's still shivering and shaking a bit from Iris, and so am I, but I'm not pulling out of my date, not on your nelly. Life goes on.

—A girl like you doesn't want to hang around with someone too clever, says Marje. —Know what I mean, Gloria? (Full of instructions, she is, the war's made her bossy.) —Don't let him French-kiss you the first time or he'll take you for a loose woman. You know what they say about the GIs and English girls' knickers, one Yank and they're –

—Ha blinking ha, I snap at her. She knows how to try and spoil your fun, she does.

Me and Marje've helped ourselves to a few nips of Dad's brandy to swallow down Iris, so I'm ready to escape into the air and leave it behind now. I'm impatient for my date, I need some laughs after seeing that arm getting blown off, and wouldn't say no to getting blotto. His name is Ron, but the way he says it, it's Raan.

—I hope he's a gentleman anyway, she says, yawning like a cat, with Mum's mouth.

Meaning she can't wait to look him over and see if she can nick him – Bobby or no Bobby. My sis wants the best for me but she wants the best for herself too, so she has what you'd call dilemmas. But I'm prettier than her, always have been. Very similar, but better-looking, because my features is regular and hers is a tiny bit conked. Except her mouth. I would like to do swaps for that mouth.

—Now sit still while I fix that hairpin. Stop wriggling, for heaven's sake. You got ants in your pants or what?

—No. Butterflies.

—In your pants? Coo-er.

Silly cow, she is. White blouse and a pink skirt, I'm wearing, with a roll-on underneath and my best undies just in case I do turn out to be loose and Marje has done my hair up lovely coiled around a sanitary towel, it's the latest gimmick she's heard of from her Wren friend, gorgeous it looks, like a doughnut, and you'd never guess what's padding it, handy too if you find you've got the curse. She sticks the last pin in and then I do the lipstick. Red lips scarlet woman, our Dad always says when he sees a girl who's no better than she should be. Putting on powder in the mirror she lets me have another squirt of the fake Chanel. Pish pish.

Ding dong.

And I'm flying to open it like I have wings, with Marje yelling after me. —Where's your bloody poise, girl? You ain't got none, is where!

But I ain't listening to nothing about poise – Marje is the world's biggest bloody expert on poise according to her – because there he is, tall on the doorstep in his airman's uniform and his blue eyes smiling at me. Off comes the little beret cap.

—Hiya, cutie! Boy, you look a million dollars, he says.

Well, of course I do. I might even be the prettiest girl in Bristol, mightn't I.

We met last week at the Red Cross dance. I spotted him right at the beginning, and he spotted me. I turned away, flirty-flirty. Then looked back. You can't help thinking Clark Gable when you see them, no matter how hard you try. No wonder the local boys are in a sulk because they can't cut the mustard next to GI Joe, one Yank and they're off, and no wonder the girls is buzzing at the factory, buzzing with the glamour. He was taller than the others and of course the best-looking, with his good-shaped head.

I was watching him while he was jitterbugging with Moira Farney's little sister. And then he was watching me doing Hands Knees Boompsadaisy.

> Hands knees and boompsadaisy,
> I like a bustle that bends.
> Hands knees and boompsadaisy,
> What is a boomp between friends?

And every time you did the boomp you had to twist your hip and boomp your bum against the other one's bum, it was like the hokey cokey but sexy-like, and he said much later on, It was your ass that attracted me first, hon. You sure had a way of twisting that butt of yours.

> Hands knees and boompsadaisy,
> Let's make the party a wow.
> Hands knees and boompsadaisy,
> Turn to your partner and bow.

And when it's over I look across and he starts making his way over to me, in his uniform, with his cocky way of walking, knows he'll get me. He doesn't hang about.

—I sure like the look of you, babe. You wanna date next week? My name's Ron.

Except he said Raan. Deep gravelly voice he's got, makes you melt.

He was right to walk like that, because I said yes, didn't I.

We did some jitterbugging together and he bought me

two gin and limes, but then I had to go, I was doing the early shift.

—See ya soon, hon, he says. —I'll come pick you up Friday.

And he was all ready to kiss me smack on the lips but I wriggled away because there was a rumour going round that the GIs thought we were easy lays and we had rounded heels from getting on our backs, and I didn't want him thinking I was one of them, did I? He looked like a speedy operator to me.

But I couldn't stop thinking about him all week, and now here he is, and my heart won't let up banging and I'm standing there gaping at him like a speechless twat, all breathless and collywobbled.

Say something, Gloria.

—Come in, I go, and a tiny voice at the back of my head whispers, *Don't do it, a bad thing is starting*, but I ignore it. Yes, even then I knew, see.

And I show him to the front room which is what Mum would've done, and we sit, and he holds out a tin with a picture of peaches on.

—Canned peaches, he says. —In syrup. Sweet syrup, cute girl. Go on, he says. —Get a can opener, have a taste.

A minute later I'm sticking my finger in the can and sucking on the syrup, and then he lifts out a big fat slice of slimy orange peach and feeds it me, and the sweet of it knocks me sideways and as it slides down my throat I'm ready to die.

—This'd cost a fortune! I go.

—They pick 'em off the trees in California, Florida, places like that, he goes. —You can have 'em any time you like back home.

I can't help it, it's been so long since I had a sweet treat, so I dip my finger in again, and suck it, and he laughs.

—There's more where that came from, hon. I'll bring you a tin of ham next time, maybe make you taste some ketchup. Ya ever have ketchup? Ketchup and fried eggs, man. Sure is good. Way better than that brown sauce shit you eat.

I have died and gone to heaven, I have.

—I've got eggs, I tell him. —Me and Marje, we keep hens.

So I am telling him about how we flog the eggs on the black market or swap them for coupons when Marje makes her entrance, and this little voice starts whispering at me again, *Bad thing, bad thing.* He stands up and holds out his hand to shake, and she looks at me and then at him, shocked that I can catch a good-looker like him because she reckons I ain't got no brains. She's right flummoxed because of this, and her famous poise goes out the window. Result being she acts like she got her tits caught in the wringer, and can't think of nothing to say except, Hello, pleased to meet you.

—This must be your sister, he says. —Boy, don't you two look alike? You could be twins! I've heard a lot about you, Marje.

Which is an out-and-out lie but it makes her blush and you can tell she likes him and I won't pretend her approval don't matter but it makes me nervy too because I don't want her liking him too much. She's not past snatching, when it's something she wants. I'm prettier, but she's the clever one.

—She's engaged to Bobby, I tell him quickly.

He and Marje just look at each other, and then I see how it must've sounded.

—Yes, says Marje. —Maybe when Bobby's back we can go out in a foursome.

—Sure, that would be swell, Marje. But tonight I'm taking this cute sister of yours to see the Great Zedorro, he says. —You know the hypnotist guy? And he waves two bits of pink. —Got tickets. Swell, huh?

Sure it's swell, with Uncle Sam's payroll and the other girls – Marje too, I'm hoping – sick with envy, you can bet. *The Great Zedorro*. He sounded famous but I'd never heard of him. I knew he was special though. That's how powerful Zedorro was. He had a hold of you before you even met him, see.

Marje is eyeing the tin of peaches.

—You ready, cutie? goes Mr Clark Gable.

Cutie! He called me cutie!

That's done it. I look at my American GI, my foreigner who says cutie, with those eyes so sparkling and clean you'd swear they were made of glass, I'm surprised he can see out of them, they look like fakes. That well-cut uniform, and his hair like a brush on top, short as short, showing off the shape of his head which is a good shape. He smiles – oh those American teeth! – and all of a sudden I'm weak at the knees. Don't ask me why, but anyway it's as quick as that, in less time than an egg takes to fry, because I know if I don't get him Marje will, so I just fall. In love I mean, then and there. Bam. One minute I'm raw, the next I'm popping and spitting and cooked. Is it the teeth? The honey and the cutie and the sister eyeing up the peaches? The name Zedorro? Is Zedorro that powerful?

—I'll go and get my coat, I go, because I have to run away for a minute.

I have to go and stand at Mum's old dressing table, looking at my flushed-up face in the mirror and breathing in out, in out, thinking: this is it. I don't even know him, but I know what love feels like now. Strange world. People in it like that, who can walk in with a tin of something sweet and grab your heart and squeeze and nearly kill you, and not even know what they've done.

15

Footsteps on the stairs, then in comes Marje, sucking her finger and smelling of peach-syrup.

—Hmm. Nice, she says. —Full marks.

—I'm not going all the way with him till I know him better, I tell her, snapping out of it, smoothing my skirt, dabbing at the lipstick. But my hand's shaking a bit.

—I should hope not! she goes. —But there's others will, you know, she says, going pish pish again with the phoney Chanel, on herself this time. —He's quite a catch.

I look up. Her blonde hair like mine, her mouth like Mum's.

—You've changed your tune, I say. It comes out sharper than I mean it to. Don't you dare, I'm thinking. Don't you dare, when I've just fallen in love, just when we're about to see the Great Zedorro.

—Pass me the lipstick, she goes, licking the peach stickiness off her lips and pouting that mouth.

That flirty face. What's she up to, making herself look nice and pishing the Chanel on herself, when it's me he's after.

—But you're not going out, are you, I say. —You're on shift soon. Lipstick's for going out. We should save it, we've only got the one, now the Revlon's buggered.

Trust her? You must be joking.

—Lipstick's for writing to Bobby, she goes, still all flirty. —I'm writing to Bobby and I'm going to put kisses in. Lipstick kisses. Then he kisses the paper just where I've kissed it.

And she makes a kissy face at us in the mirror and it's funny, she can make me laugh, and my chest eases up, because I can picture Bobby kissing her letter. That's how gone on her he is. Loony with love.

—Red lips scarlet woman, I say, and we laugh because our mum's with the angels and our dad was last heard of in Singapore and us two, we can do as we bleeding well please.

And Ron's waiting for me downstairs, and Zedorro's gearing up to dazzle us at the Little Theatre, and I don't know then about the maiming I'm in for.

THE HALLELUJAH MONSTER

—Did you ever see that famous hypnotist bloke? I ask Doris.

You never know, you could strike up a conversation with someone.

—Who? she goes, watching the weather girl waving her arms like a cockroach with its feelers.

—The Great Zedorro.

—What was he?

—What was who?

What's she on about? A lot of them have got diseases. But would it kill her to listen?

It was a red curtain at the theatre where we went to see the Great Zedorro, me and Ron. There was a big old drum-roll and then this voice that came from nowhere said, Ladies and gentlemen – the Great Zedorro! And up it went, the red curtain. All beautiful and hoopy. I didn't dare tell Ron I hadn't seen a show like this before, I'd never seen any kind of show, but I was in awe of him because he brought me a tin of peaches in syrup and he looked like a film star in his uniform.

The cymbals clashed, *da-zong*.

Then there he was on the stage, in his red cape with his black-and-white suit underneath, and red twinkly cufflinks that must be rubies, or phonies, and jet-black hair and a moustache that might be stuck on, the red curtain swishing behind him, his assistant-girl all blonde curls and red-sequinned tutu, must've cost a fortune in coupons, or she had it before the war, and stilettos. Slut Fairy was the thought that popped into my head, and Ron I noticed wasn't ashamed to be having a good old gawp. But we was all gawping if I'm being honest, filling up our eyes with the two of them in their black and white and red, all flashes and sparks.

—When they were up there on the stage, Zedorro and the Slut Fairy, it felt like our eyes was hungry, I tell Doris. But then all of a sudden there was cake.

—Cake? she goes, all excited. Her eyes pop open, wide awake. —Did you say cake?

—Not cake, goes the trolley girl, wheeling up. —First is soup, then lamb-stew-new-potato. Then trifle. If you good girls. You wanna sit here watch telly with a tray?

There is a photo in an old box, it comes from the local paper in Bristol dated 1943. It's a woman lying with her head on one chair and her feet on another chair and a big gap of nothing in the middle. The only thing that is supporting her back and her bum and her legs is Mind Control. You can do anything with your mind if you want it enough. You have to want it though. You can't just pretend to want it, your innards has to want it too. You have to be greedy for it and think it is your right, and if someone suggests it to you, such as Zedorro and his assistant the Slut Fairy, you have to think: why not, I deserve it, it ain't half bad, that idea. Bit of what happens comes from the person that does the suggesting. But most of it comes from you.

Mr Adolf H, he suggested plenty of things to the Germans. He suggested taking over France and Poland and all them countries and rounding up the Jews. And he suggested finishing them off using starvation and gas. He suggested bombing England. He made lots of happy suggestions like that, happy because they didn't seem half bad to most people, they were ordinary greedy people like you and me. Then afterwards they blamed Adolf H for brainwashing them like that, and then they had to try and forget that they ever did that stuff, and when their children found out there was a war, and asked them if they was Nazis, they shook their heads, and said, War? What war, son? There may have been one but it's just a fuzzy memory to me. I just followed orders, you would do the same.

Hank is taking me on a little outing to Gadderton Lake.
    —Fresh air'll do you good, says Hank's Wife, wiping Calum's dummy with a Wet One and popping it back in his mouth. —Look, I've done you a nice picnic.
    She sounds nice as pie, doesn't she? Hank's Wife is in actual fact called Karen but my mouth won't say it. I peek in the bag that's hanging off the pushchair and see it's smelly boiled eggs and a see-through carton of coleslaw plus Diet Coke.
    —Blow out those cobwebs, she goes. Gadderton's lovely in autumn, you'll see the bulrushes.
    —I want a couple of them buns too, I tell her. —Them currant ones.
    —Not advisable, she says. —With your duodenum, dried fruits are a strict no-no.
    —Your arse, I go. —You can pack coleslaw, you can pack a bloody bun! You starting up a one-woman rationing scheme or what, missis?
    —It's your funeral, Gloria, she says, getting out her purse and going off to the bakery.
    —That's better, I tell her when she comes back with them. —That's more like it. You are learning, you are.
    Hank is making one of his faces. You might think I hate

21

her but it's more complicated than that cos she's married to my son.

—Best visit the toilet before you go, Gloria? she says. —What with your bladder?

Meddling cow she is, she can mind her own blinking beeswax, she can blinking well go home and stew in her own juice for the day, she can –

Anyway when I have finished telling her all this, and Calum has stopped crying and got his dummy back, me and Hank get in the car and drive to Gadderton Lake where there is brambles and poplars and a Portakabin sells ices and snacks, and bright-pink maggots in plastic pots.

Hopefully there's a lav too.

Me and Hank, we're going to catch a big Hallelujah of a fish that's hiding under the skin of the water, deep down, thinking dark thoughts. There's other fishermen too, lined up under the poplars, lighting fags, adjusting binoculars, eating cheese-and-tomato sandwiches. You'd think it was the Loch Ness whatsit, but this one's got big round Jesus eyes, surprised as hell.

Oops! A flip of water. A fin or a tail. Talk of the devil.

—D'you see that? goes Hank.

Yes, I did see it, but I am wondering where you're supposed to spend a penny round here.

—We'll get the ugly bastard, goes Hank, smacking a mosquito and inspecting it. —Just you wait.

Wait?! It's OK for him to talk, he's not the one needs a wee. Some outing. You could crack a mile wide with the boredom of it, I've picked twenty-eight dandelion heads which is how bored, sitting watching him with his profile and his rod. Bright yellow, the flower splash, you'd like to squash that exact shade and pickle it in a Kilner.

To keep my mind off the wee, I think about the hypnotist, the Great Zedorro, who has been popping up in my head since my duodenum and Sea View. What I'm thinking is: he had you in his grip, and you didn't even know it. You were like this fish, when we get him. You took the bait. You swallowed. But there's a minute or two before you realise you're caught.

Tell a joke, says this little voice in my head at Gadderton Lake. *Stop you thinking about Iris and Zedorro and lavs.*

—Knock knock.

—Shhh, goes Hank. —You'll disturb him.

When I say knock knock, he's s'posed to say, Who's there? And then I'm s'posed to say, Jonah, and he's s'posed to say, Jonah who? And then I'm going to go, Jonah Ford Sierra by any chance? I always remember a joke, don't tell me I don't, I heard that one from a boy in Maddon Hill Park, Hank's Wife took me.

—Hey! yells Hank, and schloopaloop, suddenly the bobbin' thing's gone under.

—Gotcha! And he's swinging the rod up-up, and I've forgotten what was in my head before.

—You did it, Hank, you did it, my deario, and they didn't, nah-nah nah-nah nah! I'm yelling, and it's up there dripping water, the fish all Bacofoily on the line, and next he's jitterbugging on the grass and all the ciggie and sandwich fishermen are coming up to take a squiz, green with envy, you can bet.

—Quick! Quick! I've got to bash its head! goes Hank.

I'm really fighting back the wee now.

And he goes bash bash with a block of bamboo stick, bash bash, you can hear the wet slap of it, and then the blood splitters out of its gills while it's still dancing and flipping. Then something comes over me and I need a go at it too.

—Gimme a go at it, gimme a go! I go, and I'm in a frenzy of it, half falling out of the wheelchair, and I take the stick and I bash the fish too, bash it till it's well dead, no more of that flip-flopping. And then I see her. The baby.

She's in the water, floating but upright.

She is stark naked and covered in mud and weeds. She's clutching a mush of fabric in one fat hand, maybe parachute silk, and in the other fat hand a string of whitey-pink glass beads what is mine, I recognise them, *My bloody beads! Gimme them back!* and the look she's giving me, it's full of hate. *Hate hate hate. I hate you,* she's saying but silent, just saying it with the power of her thoughts. You might think a baby don't feel no hate, babies only feel love. But you are wrong because she is feeling hate all right, this one. Then she slips away again and all I can hear is the murmur of Zedorro, his voice all calm and quiet, going, *Imagine a stretch of water.*

I go wuzzy for a minute and then I try to think of a joke but I can't, so I give the fish another bash for luck, more stinky blood that's darker than you think. *Zedorro,* says a little voice in my head, as I'm bashing and bashing. *Zedorro and the Slut Fairy.*

What's happening? The men are shooting me looks, lidding up their maggots, buggering off as if I am a mad old lady gone over the top with something. Oh I get it. This here is not in real actual-factual life the famous-celebrity fish. It's a bloody blinking impostor.

—The one we were after, he was twice as big, says Hank.
—This is only medium-sized. By the way, you totally lost it there, Mum. I mean one hundred per cent. Look what you've done, its head's just pulp.

—I need a wee, I tell him, even though in fact it's too late because the chair's gone clammy and my skirt's got a stain of wet.

He didn't need to of told me it wasn't the one, did he. It looks big enough to me and now he's ripped all the glamour out of it, and the baby girl from the lake, with her mush of fabric and her beads, *Gimme them bloody beads back, you little bitch*, she has got me so shook and muddled that I can't think of a single bloody joke.

—Is there a lav round here? I go, and it comes out as a croak. Hank does this big sigh.

When we've changed my undies, which is a complicated ruddy hoo-ha even with Disabled, and the fishing gear's packed and the wheelchair's folded in the boot, it's a folding one, Hank collapses it quicker than you can blink, he's always been good with his hands ever since he was a little boy –

Where –?

Inside me there's a story about Zedorro and the Slut Fairy, a story that's screaming to say itself, worse than a joke I can't remember, worse than some food I can't lay my hands on. But I lose track, all I know is that in times of war you drop your knickers easier, but they're all civvies here, in mufti, what is called leisurewear, they're in no hurry, they don't see no wrecker balls. If you had known me in the old days you'd have said, She's not evil or even bad, she is just a girl in wartime doing war things. In fact I like her spark which is now next to nothing, just a tiny pilot light what is small and greeny-blue and trembles in the wind. In times of war you drop your knickers easier. At least I did, I won't deny it, but it wasn't like you think. I know what you're thinking if you are someone watches telly. It wasn't like that. And if I did something bad –

—Come on, now, let's get going, says Hank. —Get this customer in, and shoot off home, eh?

The impostor fish goes in the boot wrapped in the *Daily Express*. You can smell the cold greenish pond smell in the car even with the air freshener which is like a credit card that you hang from the mirror and is lavender flavour.

He's ruined the day as far as I'm concerned. Might as well have dropped a bomb on it. A doodlebug or one of them incendiaries that you can only put out with sand.

SLUT FAIRY

At the flicks in London – the Regent, cos the Scala was bombed out – they showed a newsreel of a concentration camp they'd opened up like a big old can of worms. Blimey. You wanted to close the lid on it and run away. They didn't warn you properly or nothing, about how disgusting it was going to be. They just showed it.

No one wants to be photographed or filmed not looking their best, do they? Especially not in the nude. But there they were, those poor bastards. I mean you can take being slim too far. Some of them was just limping skeletons, and some just lay there in their beds or on the floor. They was going to die, them ones, no matter what. They didn't say it on the newsreel but you could see it. They'd died long ago in their heads, the thing that was human had been sucked out of them.

One woman – I could tell she was a woman because there was the remains of tits on her chest – she looked so terrible. Even if you'd tried to improve her with a bit of nose-powder and some lipstick, and given her a nice wig for hair, she'd still have looked like a bloody nightmare. Death warmed up, she was, and her haggardy Jew eyes followed you, accusing, as if what Hitler did to her was your fault, as if you didn't have enough problems of your own to keep you awake nights.

My heart was thumping like mad, and my breathing wasn't right, so in the end I got up and barged my way along the line of seats and out into the street, where there was a bloke who left just before me, throwing up all over the pavement.

That Jew woman with the remains of tits, she didn't never let me alone after that.

I couldn't do no proper crying, so I just walked and walked, by all the bombed-out shops and houses, craters and rubble everywhere. Saw an upstairs room cut clean in half. Saw the wallpaper, and a fireplace with a mantel and a mirror above. Table looked set for a meal, plates and all, and chairs. Bit of red carpet hanging down flapping in the wind, like a busted doll's house.

Still I felt her, those eyes following me all down the street, blaming me for stuff I didn't do. I couldn't think of a joke and I got hungrier and hungrier for banana custard, tinned peaches, jam roly-poly, real oranges, all those things you couldn't get.

Sometimes in the night when I can't sleep I still see those haggardy Jew eyes. And sometimes in the day I can still feel them on me. It's like I never shook her off.

Hypnotism works like this. You get a man, it is usually a man, who has a way of looking into your eyes that reaches right clear to your soul. He tells you to do a thing you want to do anyway. You do it. And when it's done, who takes the blame?

Him?

You?

No one?

The war?

The curtain's twitching.

I know what's making it twitch. It's her. The little girl, the floating one from Gadderton, giving me the once-over.

I don't have to see her to know she's there, I can feel her sucking away on them glass beads of mine wrapped in her mush of parachute silk like an ugly little mermaid that's an abortion.

Twitch twitch.

Well, sod it, I'm calling her bluff, I am. She gave me a bit of a shock at the lake, I won't deny it, made me lose it with the dead fish. But now I know she's just one of them things happen at my age, like widdle escaping into your knickers before you reach the lav, like Zedorro and the Slut Fairy popping up out of nowhere, like catching an impostor and bashing its head to pulp, cos you got in a time muddle. Like forgetting the bloody punchline.

So she can twitch away behind that curtain all she likes, but it won't butter no parsnips with me, I can just blinking well ignore her and that is what I ruddy well plan to do.

—You hear that, young madam? I call across. —You hear what I'm planning? Cos excuse me, if anyone's a victim of atrocity, it's me.

It's quite a show. Look at him in his black and white and red, and the Slut Fairy flashing her sequins like a lit-up whore. First comes the tricks with rabbits and hats ever so slick, and then the coloured handkerchiefs which is silk-looking. Then he gets the Slut Fairy in a wood cabinet and saws her in half.

—They do this with mirrors, hon, Ron murmurs at me. —I seen it before back in Chicago.

On and on goes the sawing, with her legs at the bottom and her head at the top. And I wouldn't've grieved if that was for real the way Ron's looking at her, his eyes swooping up and down like searchlights in the Blitz. I feel like telling him when she comes out (all in one piece, but if you think about it, it'd be a much better show if she was in bits), she's wearing falsies under that blinking tutu, mate – but we're not that close yet and he might think less of me so I keep my trap shut. Anyway the cutting-in-half stuff was just to get our appetite going, because everyone knows what the Great Zedorro's speciality is, don't they, he's world-famous for his powers of Mind Control, it says so on the posters outside.

—Now are any of you ladies and gentlemen feeling the urge to come on stage? Do I have any risk-takers in the audience? goes Mr Zedorro. Anyone feel their hand ready to shoot up and say yes to something?

There certainly is, mister. It's me, and my hand's shot up, so eager it's straining the stitching in my blouse.

—Hey what's up, honey, siddown, goes Ron.

But I'm wanting this, wanting to show Ron what I am made of, which is not the same as the Slut Fairy because I can work precision tools in a factory and earn ten quid a week plus danger money, and I saw Iris blown up this morning, saw her arm and shoulder on the floor –

—Siddown, sweetie.

—No! You watch, I want to do this!

Because I am the risk-taker in the audience, aren't I. I am feeling the urge, just like the man said. I am not the only one with my hand up, but mine's the highest.

And Ron can see there's no stopping me and so I'm up there on the stage and the great Zedorro's kissing my hand like he is a romantic foreigner such as a spic.

—Please be seated on this chair. What is your name, please? Ah, right now, Miss Winstanley, have you ever been exposed to hypnotism before? There is no need to feel hesitation of any kind, because you will at all times be in control of your own destiny, as it were; all you need do is trust me. Do you trust me, do you think, Miss Double-U? Even though I am a relative stranger to you? We are taught not to trust strangers, are we not – and there is after all a war on. Yet there are times when we do. Do you feel you are in safe hands with me, Miss Double-U? Do you feel that you are in some way part of a family here? That the audience in this theatre will not let anything bad happen to you? Just as your family would protect you, should they sense any danger approaching?

And while he keeps up his patter the Slut Fairy's bringing more chairs out from behind the red hoopy curtain, and standing them in line till there's a whole little row of them next to the one I'm sitting on. And from up here I can see her legs might be better than mine but I've a bigger bust, and what's more hers is definitely fake bosoms bought in a shop, she's probably flat as a pancake underneath. I will tell Ron this later, I will.

—And now will my lovely assistant please fetch the final item? he goes.

And the Slut Fairy brings out a little stand from behind the curtain, and fetches this big glass bowl full of oranges and perches it on top of the stand. Looks lovely, it does, that strong orange colour. I count six. Feels like years since I ate one. I can feel my mouth water, even though from close up you can see they're fakes like the bosoms.

—Remember, ladies and gentlemen and Miss Winstanley, he's going. —Nobody can be hypnotised against their will and nobody can be persuaded under hypnosis to do something they don't want to do. So whatever you see Miss Winstanley here doing will be of her own free will under my direction. Do you think of yourself as suggestible, Miss Double-U?

I giggle a bit, and say —Dunno, might be. Try me then.

—So shall we, ladies and gentlemen? Should Miss Winstanley trust me, do you think?

And they're roaring yes and I'm feeling all those eyes on me. A million dollars. The Great Zedorro'd like me to stretch myself out along the row of chairs as if it's a bed, and close those beautiful eyes. So I do that, no problem.

And I will continue to follow his suggestions, thank you, Miss Double-U. Well, he goes on suggesting one thing after another, such as I will choose of my own free will to do as he says, because I am at all times perfectly safe. And none of it seems unreasonable and I'm perfectly calm, aren't I, because it don't seem unreasonable to lie down on my back on the row of chairs. It don't seem unreasonable to do the next thing he suggests to me neither. Feels like the most natural thing in the world, as a matter of fact, very do-able.

—Now, Miss Winstanley. I want you to become aware of your body transforming itself into . . .

Then he pauses and whispers, very intense —*A rod of iron.*

You can hear the audience suck in their breath and do some wondering – but me I'm in no doubts, because straightaway I let this big bold feeling of weight and power creep up on me from somewhere inside, and I am for the first time in my life certain of what it feels like to be not flesh but metal. Nothing simpler. What's more, I am not just any rod of iron, I am the best, strongest and most rigid rod of iron there ever bloody was.

So not unreasonable to stay like that while a drum-roll sets up from somewhere nearby, and Zedorro and the Slut Fairy start taking away the chairs, one after another, from in between my head and my feet. No trouble, what with being so rigid. I can feel the chairs going, first one under my shoulders then a second from under my knees till there's just one left under my bum, and then the drum-roll gets louder and I feel the chair slide away and hear a big old gasp from out there, because there I am, a human rod of iron, head on one chair, feet on another, nothing in the middle except Zedorro's Mind Control what I have agreed to.

It is good to feel all those eyes on me. I feel calm, like I did in the factory when Iris's shoulder got ripped out of its socket.

—Now I am going to place this heavy bowl of oranges on Miss Double-U's stomach, he goes. —As you can see, she is in a state of rigidity. She is perfectly conscious of her state, and she remains in it of her own free will.

The drum-roll sets up again and when it reaches a pitch some cymbals clash and I feel the bowl park on my belly, and hear another gasp and a wow from the stalls. But as I'm still a rod of iron, it don't make no difference to me, it ain't no weight, as the oranges are phonies, made of papier mâché or something what is hollow.

—*Voila!* goes Zedorro, and I suppose he and the Slut Fairy now takes a bow, because there is clapping and whistles and catcalls.

Is it the oranges that's impressing them? Could be, because real one's'd set you back well over two bob a pound on the black market, but no, it's really me that's getting them all worked up. I mean how often do you get to see a thing like that? I have to keep my eyes shut of course or the spell will be broken, but I hear a pop and there's a little white flash so someone has taken a picture, that I do know. A photograph of Miss Double-U the human rod of iron with a bowl of fake oranges on her belly.

Ooh and aah, I'm hearing. His voice calms you down.

—What you are witnessing here, ladies and gentlemen, is the power of auto-suggestion . . . Now very importantly, I can make this subject emerge from the hypnotic state at any time by a simple snap of the fingers . . . Miss Double-U here can hear my voice and everything I am saying to you but it is her choice to remain rigid for as long as I ask her to . . .

This is the life, I thought.

Then, too soon, I can feel the bowl being taken off my tummy and the chairs being slid back underneath me one by one, and then he says. —You may now return to your normal state, thank you, Miss Winstanley, and the minute

he says that I am all flopped again, a bit jelly-like, it feels, after being a rod of iron.

Then I'm to stand up, and show the ladies and gentlemen that I am back to normal again, so that's what I do, and I give a little wave, and try to see where Ron's sitting so's I can blow him a kiss, but I can't spot him with the lights, and the cymbals clash again, *da-zong,* for quiet.

—The power of Mind Over Matter, says Zedorro.
—Salute it, ladies and gentlemen. It is willpower that will help us through this war, the willpower of ordinary men and women like Miss Winstanley here. What you have seen tonight is not a miracle, it is more than that.

He stops and looks around, makes sure they're listening.

—What Miss Winstanley has personified for us tonight is nothing other than the triumph of the British spirit!

Well, they love this old bollocks, don't they, because they're whooping and clapping and God Save the King-ing, and everyone stands, and there we are on the stage, me and Zedorro and the Slut Fairy, celebrating Mind Over Matter, and me feeling special, like from this moment on, my life will not be the same because I have according to Zedorro boosted the war effort by being a human rod of iron and helping morale with fake oranges.

—You looked so cute, he said later, once I'd told him all about the Slut Fairy's false tits.
—How cute?
—Real hot.

He sounded like the flicks.

—How real hot?
—This real hot, he'd go, and we'd be at it again, cos it was our private secret, our own little country where only Ron and me spoke the secret filthy lingo.

We have our tea early, so the cook woman can go home and do it all over again for her family. I've found myself

34

a nice chair, it's the chair of an old bird who croaked a week ago but I don't believe in ghosts and even if I did I wouldn't fuss. The little kid from Gadderton Lake, she's still loitering behind the curtain near the tropical-fish tank, you'd get a good view of it from there, see them flitting about like little underwater fireworks. Every now and then one of them ends up floating. They bloat out when they die, full of the gas of death.

Hank shows up after Doris has spilt her stew and the news, where bad things is always happening. I don't watch it myself, I'd rather not know, thanks.

—Hi, Mum, nice sleep then?

They're showing this heart-and-lung transplant girl's birthday party on telly, but he wants to talk about this bit of paper he's waving.

—I'd like to take over power of attorney. It's all been drawn up by the solicitor. Thought it was time I dealt with your admin, if you've no objection. What with the stroke and your memory going. Here's a pen, there we go, and here are your reading specs, that's it, pop them on. I'm off on the rigs again, two weeks on, two weeks off, so I'm getting a few bits and bobs sorted before I go. If you'd like to sign? We'll need a couple of witnesses. 'Scuse us, Mrs Manyon? he calls over. —Care to do the honours here?

But Mrs Manyon – she's the one in charge of the darkies here who natter in corridors, some are thin and some are fat – she's busy.

—That old boy she's seeing to, I tell him, name of Ed Mayberley, he's pushing ninety, he was a POW in Japan like Dad. He can't keep his hands to himself, he can't. Yesterday I saw him grabbing one of the foreign girls. She nearly screams the place down and slaps him. It's abuse, that. Someone should report her.

35

He's put the bits of paper in front of me, fanned out on the tray. It looks official.

—When you're ready, Mrs M? he goes.

Now when I see the papers like that, looking official, some little voice from somewhere inside me tells me, *This signing lark is not a one hundred per cent good idea, Gloria*, but I can feel the little girl's eyes on me, boring their way in like two drills, and I can't think of a joke.

So when Mrs Manyon comes over with a pen and the new care assistant fresh in from the Philippines, I scribble my name quick to get rid of her, and the Philippine girl pretends to read the writing and she signs too, in big letters, Conchita la Paz.

She can't be more than twelve.

—Anything to eat round here? I go. Because all of a sudden I could devour an entire bloody horse.

What happens when you get hypnotised is nothing you don't want to happen, that's what Zedorro said, and he wasn't lying, he wasn't no con-man or nothing, he was just a bloke had certain useful powers. It's not like he was Hitler, hypnotising a whole bloody nation into stirring up a world war. The truth is that I had never thought about being a human rod of iron before, but when he suggested it to me I wanted to be one. And thanks to him having the idea, and me liking it, between us, him and me, and the Slut Fairy, we held a whole theatreful of people spellbound. And to anyone who says that's a crime, I say bollocks. Hitler was a criminal. The people who followed his orders, they was criminals. But me and the Slut Fairy and Zedorro, we was just three small people living in evil times. You try to go making any comparisons about the rod of iron thing and anything else that happened later, to me or anyone else, and you are sick and mad.

*   *   *

—Did you hear what Marty Lone said about his mum the other day? says Doris. She means Rubber-Lips, the Gay Homosexual. —Still tucks him up in bed if he's feeling poorly, she won't let another woman near him.

—I was like that with Hank when he was a boy. Did everything for him. Tied his shoelaces and combed his hair and put plaster on his knees when he fell off his bike. Helped him with his Airfix models and took him fishing because he didn't have no dad.

Her granddaughter's sent a box of chocs, she's been bragging about it but she's not sharing. She's picking out all the orange ones first.

—Did you sign that piece of paper then? she goes. —Because you shouldn't of, you've signed away your rights.

She's talking nonsense but it's wormed its way in, and next thing I know I've called the Welsh nurse.

—Anything I can get you there, Gloria? she goes.

—Has someone reported you yet? I go. —For attacking poor old Ed? Because it's called abuse.

—Cup of tea? Coffee?

—I saw what you did. I saw that slap.

—Leave off, Gloria, goes the decrepit one. —Maja's a good girl and anyway she's not Welsh, are you, love, you're just a foreigner.

—From Croatia.

—It's Abroad, goes the decrepit one. —They had a war there, didn't they, love? Is it over, or is it one of them ones goes on and on?

—Two my brother disappear, one uncle. Tea, coffee?

—Tea, we both say, simultaneous.

—She's got a bun in the oven, I whisper to Doris while the girl pours a cuppa.

—Really? goes D, all smiles. —Is it true you're pregnant, dear?

Ooh, you should see her face. She barely finishes pouring, then crashes off, knocking over some old creature's drip.

—Gloria, do you have second sight or something?

And I say —Yes, as a matter of fact I do.

But a bad feeling's squirming about inside me, and I could do with my mum, and Marje, and Hank's Wife making chips in the kitchen, and me and Calum cuddled up on the sofa watching *Teletubbies*.

It's the night and she's there. The little girl. She was smaller last time, she was just practically a baby, but now she's older, about four or five, wearing a yellow pinafore dress with just a little smear of mud and a plosh of pond-weed on it. Hair dripping wet. Sitting right on the bed with these whitey-pink beads made of glass that string together on a long string, they're mine, I know it, I found them on a bomb-site in London and I'm thinking: *gimme*. She's working like billy-o, stringing together one and then another and then another, very industrious, you'd think it was factory work. She don't look up. Don't give a stuff. She's obviously not the type you can tell a joke to.

—Piss off, I tell her. —Go boil your nitty head.

But she don't go, don't say nothing neither. I get the creeps then so I shut my eyes and when I open them again she's buggered off but there's a dent on the bed where she sat.

—Wanna smoke, hon? he says outside the theatre, with his packet of Lucky Strikes.

—I don't smoke, I go. —I don't know how.

If Mum was there, she'd say, And you don't want to know how, my girl, it is the beginning of a slippery slope, ciggies are for the men, you don't want to look mannish.

Old-fashioned, see. But she ain't there, is she, and Ron's laughing and pulling out two ciggies.

—Want me to teach ya? he goes, waving one at me, circling it, then popping it in my mouth like a thermometer. I can feel the paper of it.

—You mustn't laugh if I cough, I go, my lips clenched on it. He looks me in the eyes all serious. —Promise you won't?

—Honey. Cross my heart and hope to die, I won't laugh at ya, babe. Now when I hold the flame to it, you suck the air in, but don't inhale. Just take some air into that cute little mouth, like this. (He shows me, it looks easy enough.) —Then blow out the smoke. Let's see ya do it.

I did what he said.

I coughed of course, and he laughed like he promised not to. But the next puff I didn't cough, and it was fine after that. That was my first ciggie. I didn't think much of it, but I came to like it and by the end of the war I was a chimney, wasn't I.

There was other things I came to like too.

All the people was streaming out of the theatre, out into the deep dark of the street.

I'd had boyfriends before the war of course and I've always liked men and they've always liked me. But I felt new with Ron, like what happened in the theatre with the Great Zedorro made it special even before it began. In the street where we first kissed after we'd stamped out the ciggies, there was a hot-water bottle slashed open as if someone'd taken a knife to it. As he was kissing me I'd open one eye from time to time and look at that hot-water bottle, like it was an anchor to keep me from floating up into the sky like a balloon on the gush of rum and smoke and man-smell that was his kiss, and this time there was no little voice whispering, *No, Gloria, don't do it*, or if there was it was drowned out by another voice saying, *Yes, Gloria, do*.

I knew I wouldn't be a virgin for much longer the way I was feeling, and him too, pressing against me, and you could feel the hardness.

Yes, Gloria, do.

On the way home we saw searchlights swinging across the low clouds, and there was this bright glow on the road that was its reflection. Then all of a sudden the lights went out, just like that, and we were left in the pitch dark. We stood still, holding hands, and then kissing. Snogging our faces off, we were, and my knickers was getting looser by the second, I can tell you.

When we stopped to breathe he said, —Hey, this is different, isn't it, Miss Gloria Double-U.

And I said. —Different? I should coco.

—I was just a cog in one hell of a big fucking war machine.

We're swaying because we're a bit drunk and maybe even then a bit in love, walking through the blackout together. I can't believe what a dirty mouth he has, but the swear words are different from English ones, they're right sexy. I've told him about the Lousy Nitwit factory, and now he's telling me about how he got here.

—I was working with my old man in our gasoline station back in Chicago, fixing cars out the back, that's what we did, we pumped gas and fixed automobiles. I didn't want to be no fuckin' cannon fodder. But shit, along came Pearl Harbor and I thought: hey. That's it, man. Soon as I heard that news I enlisted. Did my Ninety-Day Wonder and my pilot's training and shipped out here in November last year. Then went to Tunisia.

Tooneesia, it sounded like.

We walk along a bit more and then stop and kiss some more and then he starts tickling me and I get the giggles, and tell him the joke about the wide-mouthed frog, and when he stops laughing he says to me —Gee, I sure get a bang outa the way you guys talk.

—I'm a cockney, me, so's Marje, we're not Bristol people. We don't talk like the others, we got teased at school.

—Well, you Brits all sound the same to me, he goes. —You came from London, huh?

—When I was twelve and Marje was fourteen. Our dad worked in meat in Cheapside, but he and Mum wanted to move to Bristol, better hours on the buses, see. But I'm a Londoner, me, I'm going back there one day. Soon as I can, soon as the war's over. Now go on, tell me about *Tooneesia*.

He thinks for a bit.

—That desert was so darn cold, man, he goes. —You lay in your tent two hours before dawn, thinking: I've never been so miserable in my whole goddamn life. You put all the blankets on top of you, you ache from how hard the ground is. You put some underneath, you freeze your ass off. But when the sun comes up, boy, it's like the American West! Real Technicolor. White sand and this green desert grass, it's like Arizona or somewhere. He spits out his gum and it lands with a tiny splat in the dark. —But back home they don't have no Ayrabs.

Me and Doris is watching this new game show called *I Must Confess*. There's families and some of them is bluffing about the bad things they did and some is not, and if you win you get a thousand quid. But the host man, he says squids, as in, A thousand squids, ladies and gentlemen.

Then in walks Hank's Wife who is having an affair, every Thursday he comes to do the business. He's got one of them red cars with eyelids, I heard her tell him I've got Mad Cow, *Her mind's a sieve*, was her words.

Hank thinks he is her accountant of course, accountant my arse.

—Bought a little pressie for you, says Hank's Wife, and plonks this little bag in my lap that's got a drawstring.

—You should go on that programme, I tell her. —Confess your sins. You could win us some dosh.

But she's pretending not to hear, fussing with the baby, who's crawling about on the floor getting his dummy all fluffed up, my Hank never had a dummy. Know something? There wasn't a better baby than Hank in all the world. And not a better boy than Hank and not a better man, she don't deserve him, she don't.

—Are you going to have a look then, Gloria?

The bag's made of fake silk which is red and Chinesey. There's stones in it.

—Semi-precious, she says. —Healing Stones, they're the latest thing. I've ordered some for the shop. You hold them in your palm and they calm your mind. Re-energise you. I'm so glad you've settled in. It's a lovely home, isn't it? Nice carers, lovely view –

—Do I look like I need bloody sodding stuffing blinking re-energising? It comes out loud, louder than I thought I could shout, because the blood's rushing about now. No stopping it. —Handful of bloody pebbles is all they are, look! Load of old rubbish!

I've chucked the lot at the window, and it splits across with a big crack. Then all the air from outside is whooshing in, it smells of frankfurters from the harbour, there's a van does them.

—Healing, my arse. Healing, my flaming arse!

Next thing the little pregnant nurse is on the scene saying —Calm down, please, Gloria, all she do, she come give you nice present, you go break window! I tell Mrs M!

Calum starts screaming the place down like a spoilt brat. If there's one thing I hate it's a baby.

—I'm the closest you'll ever get to having a daughter, goes Hank's Wife.

—Who says I wanted one, eh? Who ever bloody says I wanted one?

I'm shouting cos the Hoover's started up.

—Time to say bye-byes to Granny, Calum. Upsy-daisy, off we go.

—Girls are nothing but trouble, I tell Doris when Hank's Wife has buggered off. —They get pregnant. Vicious circle.

—My granddaughter isn't trouble, she says.

—So where is she, I go, Timbuktu?

—Rushed off her feet, she's got five, and two under seven. She sent me these chocs though, see? Just what the doctor ordered.

You'll notice she's mentioned them again. Rubber-lips comes on and we both spot he's looking peaky but think nothing of it, just that he might have a bit of a temperature. When the Hoovering stops and the window's been taped up, the curtain starts twitching again. But she still don't come out.

—No one's that shy nowadays, I tell Doris. —It's not the fashion.

But Doris is off with the fairies, staring straight ahead of her with a choc melting in her hand.

—There's an Englishman, Irishman and a Scotsman, I tell her. —They've all done crimes, so they go to jail for twenty years but they're allowed to take in one luxury, so the Englishman, he takes loads of women, the Scotsman takes loads of whisky, and the Irishman he asks for a million cigarettes. After twenty years they're all released and the press is there asking how it was. The Englishman, he can hardly walk he's been having it away so much with all them women, but he's got a big smile on his face. Great, he says. Then the Scotsman he staggers out blind drunk. How was it, they ask, and he's too pissed to answer but he's happy as Larry. Then out comes the Irishman, who wanted all of them ciggies. And d'you know what he says to all them people? He says, Have you got a light there now?

That's a funny one, my sis Marje came back from night-shift with it.

But Doris don't laugh. She just stays sitting there, with the melted choc in her hand, staring straight ahead like a blinking statue.

—You should get some air, Doris, I tell her. —Just look at you. Your face is all white.

BLUE-EYED BOY

The Great Zedorro had an effect on us, a sex effect. No mistaking it. We'd always joke about it, we'd talk about a Zedorro Moment, that was our secret code for it. I wanna give you a Zedorro Moment, hon, he'd say, hand sliding up my skirt, rum and ciggies on his breath, that tang of American aftershave mingled in, or sometimes in the evenings his stubble would be growing back cos of being a hairy bugger and his chin would scrape my skin like sandpaper, the roughest kind of sandpaper, and my face would be red from it afterwards, like mutilation.

Anyway after that first kiss when I looked at the hot-water bottle and he walked me home through the blackout, I asked him in and we sat on the settee together having a bit of a snog. Marjorie was on shift, and the house was ours, Mum and Dad staring down at us from the mantelpiece, I nearly turned them to face the wall and then I thought: no, you're gone now, this is my life, I can do what I want, and you can blinking well watch.

He's a talker, my blue-eyed airman. As in, you can't get a bloody word in – but I'm happy to listen. Don't understand half of what he says, but that's not the point, is it. The point is that it's like being with a real live film star.

—Those P-38s we flew in Tunisia, they're rugged ships, man. This buddy of mine, he was strafing some trucks and he came in to attack so low he hit his right wing against a telephone pole. Any other plane, that wing would've come off right there. Hitting the pole that way flipped him over on his back, and he was flying upside-down ten feet off the ground.

He drops my hand so he can show me the movements.

—He gripped that stick so hard the inside of his hand was black and blue for a week afterward. And you know what? She came right side up and he flew her home.

I'm about to say something but he's off again.

—See, any one-engine plane would have slipped and crashed into the ground. But the thing about those two counter-rotating props is, they do one hell of a job when it comes to eliminating torque.

My hand's on his knee and I'm thinking: what's torque, and suddenly he notices me again.

—You sure are cute, honey, he goes. Then he laughs to himself, and his blue eyes get this glitter in them. —You know how long it's been since I did this? And he's pressing on my right tit.

But I don't want to know, do I, because it's probably only a week or so, and anyway I'm not interested in them other girls he had, I'm interested in him and me. So the snogging and smooching turns to more like heavy petting and he's got my blouse unbuttoned, my bra undone – you can tell he's an expert – and my tits out, he's kissing them all over like they're precious and he can't decide which one's the best, rolling his tongue around the nipples, and it gives me this jabbing tingle that spreads like fever or one of them electric storms, so that I'm three-quarters of the way towards you-know-whatnot, it could happen any time if I just let it, but I want that thing of his in me first.

—Come to bed, I'm gasping, can't even speak properly I'm that gone, my tongue's glue.

But we don't even get that far, do we. He's slid down on to the floor and I'm still on the sofa, and he's pushing my

46

legs apart and sliding his way up and my roll-on's stretched to the limit until suddenly he's shoved it right up round my waist and my legs are free and my undies are off and my tits is being squeezed and licked at again and after a bit of hopping about his trousers are off and he's showing me this thing of his. Which is strange to look at, because I haven't seen one in the flesh before, just little boys' ones, which is not the same. Anyway, this thing, which looks to me a little bit like one of them toadstools with a long stalk called a stinkhorn from The World of Fungus, it belongs inside me, that much I do know.

Next thing – no time to think or say nothing – he's jammed it in there, so painful, right to the hilt, and I'm gasping like a fish.

They turn up at tea-time and park the hearse in the forecourt. You can hear them but not see them because they've drawn the curtains, which they must have the habit of, in a place like this. I don't go near them curtains myself, because of the Gadderton girl hiding in the folds somewhere, but I get Ed to pull one side back a bit so's we can take a peek.

—There you go, my darling, he says. —Anything for a lady.

That's when I take a look at him, and I notice he's not such an ugly old codger for his age, even though you can see the splashes of different colour on the skin of his head, and he's in a wheelchair most of the time and his hearing-aid screams when you get close.

Not bad.

—Well, he says. —They didn't stint on the flowers, did they.

I used to be a swell kid, I'm thinking. So when's he going to spot it then?

But he's too busy because of Doris. White flowers, loads of them, on the coffin, them reeky ones that pollinate your clothes, can't get the orange off even with a dry-clean at Mr Speedy's, ten pounds minimum for a two-piece. Puffed-up men in hats and black regalia, what a miseryguts job. Mrs Manyon lording it, fussing about with the relatives.

—Blessed release really, she says, with that last set of scans. You don't want to put them through chemo at her age, it's downright cruel plus the state can't really afford it when there's kids queuing up for kidneys and whatnot. Sometimes things are best left to Mother Nature.

There's one lady there looks like she must be the granddaughter, five she's got and two under seven, and another one her husband who's maybe in Personnel. He's holding her by the arm like she's a barrel with a special handle. She might keel over, but she don't. They get in a black car and drive off behind the coffin one.

She's the one who sent the chocs which was Doris's booby prize.

—I hope I die in the lilac season, I tell Ed. —Cos there's no beating lilac.

—I was just remembering that film, goes Ed. —*Road to Morocco*. It was Bob Hope and Bing Crosby and Dorothy Lamour. She had that touch of the Dorothy Lamours, our Doris.

As soon as he's said that I hear something right next to me. It's Doris, laughing.

—D'you hear that? I ask Ed. But he's turned to look at the Welsh girl's tits and I'm on his deaf side.

—Are you there, Doris? I whisper over the scream of Ed's deaf-aid.

There's this tinkly shiver chasing up and down my spine. Silence, but I know she's there. Her and the Gadderton girl, laughing at what Ed just said, and laughing at Mrs Manyon, and laugh-laugh-laughing at the funeral man and all the tommyrot that's in store for her in church.

*   *   *

—I'm off on the rigs tomorrow, Mum, came to say good-bye, says Hank. —Thanks for signing the paperwork.

—That Wife of yours still hasn't apologised. You should make her say sorry.

—Her name's Karen. And I think you're the one owing an apology.

—They were just a handful of bloody pebbles. Could've got them on the beach.

When he has buggered off I just sit there, listening to the hum in my head getting louder and louder, till I have to jump off a cliff in my head, into a sleep that is dark green like Gadderton but bottomless.

Well, it was quite an experience, that first bit of whatchermacallit that me and Ron got up to on the settee there. Fooling around, he called it. As in, Wanna fool around again, hon? Not at all what I'd expected, from what Marje'd said, even though she'd given me the gory details about what Bobby had done to her in places like the coalshed. Not as bad as I thought it would be – and you could even begin to see how if it wasn't too painful you could get to like it, just like ciggies. Our mum would've had a heart attack if she could've known what we were getting up to, but she was gone, wasn't she, no one there to say to us, You mark my words, girls, you will come a cropper.

And that body of his, it was like one of them statues of a god you see in them pictures from Ancient Greece, but with hair, hair on his tummy and chest and a whole gluey nest of it where his thing lay, all shrunked and shrivelled now. I look for a long time, and then I can't resist touching so I slide my hand ever so gently down his flat belly that is breathing soft and has a sheen of sweat, because I want to touch that magical stinkhorn thing of his again and see if it will go hard in his sleep. But he senses something and flips sideways and wriggles into a new position – and it's then I see it.

A huge ugly scar, on the side of his thigh.

It's purple and jagged and it shocks me right through. There's stitching marks that's purple and not well done, and I realise he never told me nothing, it was all about his buddies as he called them, and who got shot down and killed on what mission, and who had a close shave.

I nudge him awake and point at the scar.

—How d'you get it?

He laughs, all sleepy.

—You like it, hon? Doc did a real good job, eh. He was a British guy. Yeah, I was invalided out for a while there, man. Damn near lost my leg.

He starts humming a tune, 'Blue Skies'. So relaxed, lying there on the floor in the candle-light, the two of us. His hand on my belly, mine stroking the scar. I shut my eyes and he starts singing the words in his gravelly voice. All out of tune he is, but so what.

> Blue skies smiling at me,
> Nothing but blue skies do see.
> Bluebirds, singing their song,
> Nothing but bluebirds from now on . . .

Then he turns and kisses me, and I kiss him back.

—So how did it happen? Is it a war secret?

I kiss the scar; his skin is salty.

—No, it's no secret, hon, ain't gonna have no secrets from you, sweetheart. I'd just shot down this Junker 52, that's a troop carrier. And bam, before I could even congratulate myself, these Messerschmitts start attacking. So I'm putting some altitude between us, and then there's this big crack and a shell hits the windshield.

I kiss him all over while he's talking, I want to kiss it all away.

—I don't know what the fuck happened. It must've got deflected through the top of the canopy and down on the instrument panel – anyways, I get hit in three places, left chest – there was a scar here, hon. He takes my hand and puts it to his chest, and I feel a small ridge under the hair. —Oh, plus left arm.

He shows me a dent. —And left thigh.

I wipe the wet off my face and kiss the thigh-scar again.

—So what did you do? I say, looking up. I can't imagine this, even after Iris.

—Well, I know right away the thigh wound's real bad, so I drop my belly tank and get the ship under control, then head for home. Put a tourniquet on my leg, gave myself a shot with the hypodermic, and took sulfanilamide tablets right there in the ship. Don't know how I did it, just followed my training, I guess. Landed at my own base one hour later. Got out the cockpit, walked maybe three yards, then just collapsed. Woke up in the hospital, with the doc saying, I don't know if we can save your leg, Lieutenant Taylor.

I breathe, my head rested on his tummy, my face right next to his thing that's asleep. And then he's stroking my hair and running his hands through it —You've got such beautiful hair, sweetheart – and the stroking gets sort of thicker and he is pushing my head down and then I get the idea that it is my mouth he wants there, it don't seem like such a bad thought, and so with his hands doing the explaining I put my lips around and it's straightaway growing like a miracle plant and the groaning noises he is making, they are the happiest groans I have ever heard and it works me to a wild pitch too, just knowing the effect it's having. So with his hands on my head and his fingers tangled in my hair, we do it another way.

Afterwards he kisses the top of my head and smears what I've spat out across his tummy and rubs it into mine like body lotion and says I'm a real A-1 honey, and rolls over and sings more 'Blue Skies', lullabying himself to sleep with his gravel voice.

> Never saw the sun shining so bright,
> Never saw things looking so right.
> Noticing the days hurrying by,
> When you're in love, my how they fly . . .

And a minute after that he's breathing the way he does when he's asleep, gentle and quiet as anything, leaving me all lonely and in awe, because those dangers he'd passed, they made me love him more. Blue days all of them gone.

OLD NAZI

—Twinkle twinkle, little star. What you say is what you are. I am singing the kid a song, see, who says I am not fit to be a mother? There's an old mop leaning against the wall, that's been mopping up blood. The mop is red from the blood because the blood is fresh, and it's all over me and all over the baby. And Zedorro, he's hovering in the air in his black cape like a vampire above us, and when he smiles you can see his bloodsucking fangs. Under the cape he's wearing a white utility shirt that cost seven coupons from Hope's. The Slut Fairy's there too. She's lurking in the shadows like a snake waiting to steal an egg. Zedorro's getting ready to rip flesh and suck blood.

—There's blood in that mop if you want some, I tell him.
—Keep away from me. Suck the mop.

But he flies down lower and lower.

—Suck the mop! Suck the mop! Suck the mop!

A whining woman is there too, whining about the thing she has lost, going: I need to find her, I need to find her and tell her how I have lived my whole life with a part of me missing, a part of me missing, a part of me missing. I am like half a person, I have always been half a person, and without my other half I can never be whole . . .

*   *   *

53

—Calm down now, Gloria. Bad dream? I'll adjust this drip here and then when Dr Sharma's had a look at you, you can have another nice rest.

I'm rubble. Feels like something's slid off down or sideways in my head, got lost down the back of it like something down a sofa, can't be bothered to get it back, the furniture's shifted about, there's stuff that was at the bottom come to the top and stuff that was at the top slid to the bottom.

—You took a little turn for the worse, Gloria, says the brown doctor. —How are you feeling?

—Stabbed in the back.

—What was that?

—I had no choice, did I.

—Try and have a sleep. You'll feel better after some rest.

—She was asking for it! I tell him, but the door has closed.

—They're busy men, says the nurse, making a face.

—Are you in love with him?

She snorts.

—Dr Sharma? You must be joking! He's old enough to be my father!

—Does he pay you for sex?

—Let me sort out this pillow, she says, as if she hasn't heard.

—You should charge them, I tell her. —They can always pay a bit more than you think, especially if you'll do American things. Sucking cocks and that. Take it from me, love.

But the room's gone quiet.

I'm teaching Marje to smoke, cos she's got her knickers in a twist about Bobby. There's been no letters for a week. Bobby's an airman, like Ron. He does them raids on Germany, like they does to us, but less now. When we see a plane going over, I know what she's thinking. She's thinking: if this was Germany, that might be Bobby. That plane might get attacked, the pilot might be killed, or he might have to parachute out. She's forever counting the formations out and counting them back in again, and every time there's one missing – sometimes more – she's a nervous wreck.

Smoking's s'posed to calm you down, but not the way she does it. She takes to it even faster than I have, masters it quicker, holds the ciggie like Greta bloody Garbo of course, she ain't as pretty as me but she knows how to hold herself because of her poise thing.

—I bought an old parachute yesterday, she tells me, puffing out smoke. The hens is pecking around our feet out in the yard.

—What for? How much?

—Swapped six eggs and five clothing coupons with Deirdre's mum. Want to see it? I'll show it you.

And out she goes and comes back with this hump of cloth, slippy and thin when you touch it. It looks ghosty.

—I'll use Mum's sewing machine, she says, smoothing out a bit. —I've got a pattern.

—I'd be superstitious, I say, fingering it.

It's heavier than it looks.

—If I've got the wedding dress, I'll have the wedding, she snaps. —Soon as the war's over, and Bobby's home, and Dad's back. We'll have a big family wedding.

We haven't got no big family, but Bobby has. They're from round Redland, he and Marje were sweethearts from way back. Then they broke up cos she fancied another bloke but then she found out the other bloke was already married to a girl in Sheffield who was up the duff, and then the war came and everyone signed up and she and Bobby got back together, and she ain't a virgin no more, I can tell you, after a certain moment in the coalshed followed by many more moments in all sorts of places including our hen-house, she told me once, must've forgot her poise that day. He's a good-looking boy, got a touch of the spic about him with his dark hair and flashing eyes and big laugh, you could picture him with a cutlass and a parrot on his shoulder and a yo-ho-ho. He asked her to marry him the night before he went away, and she didn't want him dying without knowing the feel of her body, did she.

She sits down crumpling the parachute up in her lap, face all dreamy, thinking of herself in that wedding dress.

I might borrow that dress off her one day, I'm thinking. For my own wedding. To Ron. That's a happy moment, that is, the two of us out in the yard dreaming our silly dreams.

An ambulance comes.

—Your taxi, madam, says the driver, wheeling the bed in. —Come to take you home.

Where's that, I'm wondering. Bristol? Tooting? Chicago?

—Sea View, he says. His face is red and blue, all mottled like a lobster. I had a client like him in Balham, Mr Loomis, he was generous to me.

—Know any jokes?

He thinks for a minute.

—What d'you call a mushroom that walks into a bar and buys everyone a drink?

—What?

—A fun guy to be with, he goes. —Fungi, as in mush-room. Get it?

Get what?

Sea View, and sure enough there is a view of the sea, a little wedge of grey-blue through the window of the lounge. There's an up-your-arse matron in charge, can't remember her name any more, doesn't matter. Then this woman turns up with a little boy, a toddler.

—How're you feeling, Gloria? she goes.

But I'm watching the little boy, I've seen him before, he used to spit out his custard, muck up the lino with it. Every day he'd do that, or turn a whole bowl of good mashed potato and gravy upside-down, and if his father was around he would probably say, Jesus, Gloria, can't you teach that kid some goddamn control, for Chrissake?

In his American accent.

—How old is he then? I ask the woman who looks familiar.

—Nearly two.

—Younger than I thought, I thought he'd be fifty by now, I thought he'd be approaching retirement.

—Nice view, from this wing, she goes, because we're staring out. —Are you feeling more yourself now?

—I was hungry the whole time in the war, so was Marje. We used to watch the hens laying and pounce on them eggs, we could've eaten them raw we were that desperate.

—Hank's still on the rig, she says, but he sends his love. He's sorry you've been poorly.

Rig? I'm wondering but I can't be arsed and I let it pass. But it nudges the back of my head like bad medicine. What's a baby boy doing on a bloody rig?

I must've been asleep for quite a while because the Welsh nurse, her bump's well established now, there's no hiding it.

—You getting married, then? I call. —Or won't his wife divorce him?

You can tell her sort, I know it better than I know myself. But she doesn't even blush, she just pretends not to hear, she's learned bad habits.

I want to warn her: Love can kill you, you know. Or if it doesn't, it can leave you half dead. Did you ever see a building site with one of them wrecking balls, they hang it from a crane and they swing it, bash down ceilings and walls that was once a house? Love will probably kill you, see. And if it doesn't, you'll be maimed like Iris, or you'll end up like me.

Full of holes.

I don't like the news but sometimes I watch by accident and when I do it always has a bad effect on me. Who do they think they are, coming on and depressing everyone like that?

Today there's a man who was a war criminal, he was a guard at one of the death camps. Eighty thousand people were gassed there, but they weren't wanting to do him for the gassing, it was about some prisoners they say he shot for fun. It's worse, if you do it for fun and it's not part of your regular job. He's eighty-something and he is blind and he has cancer but he's looking well on it. It all happened when he was young, just late teens, early twenties, and he said his support for Hitler was a youthful indiscretion. He's denying he did the killing of course, and the Jew man is saying that's making it worse, because the first crime is the first crime, he says, but the second crime is the crime of denial. You hide your crime, you deny the past, or you forget the evil you did, forget it on purpose, and you're committing another atrocity.

And Ed's saying —Yes yes, the man's right, he should be hanged. —By the neck, he adds, in case we're confused. —Those Jap guards in the camp, they weren't hardly human, some of them. I don't care if they was only following orders. Anyone can say that, can't they. Oldest trick in the book. And then what does Mr Jap do? Pretends it never happened. Won't say sorry because it'd lose him his precious bloody face. All swept under the carpet.

See what I mean about the news? It gets people worked up, they shouldn't show it in homes where people is old and fragile. It's not just Ed who's getting in a tiz neither.

I'm getting these crawly thoughts again, cos I know there's a connection between a certain this and a certain that, but I'm buggered if I know what it is. I am getting hungry and in need of a joke, but I can't think of one and I am ready to explode with something, I am.

—Let bygones be bygones, Ed! He's another person now, he ain't a Nazi no more, he's just a man. Probably grows potatoes in his back garden and if he wasn't blind he'd probably watch TV same as the rest of us! Look at him, he's got cancer for God's sake. And he's paid his dues, he's forgotten what he did, we should forget it too. It's more than fifty years ago; give the man a bloody break, won't you?

My heart's banging away like the clappers, feels it might crack my ribs. Don't know why it matters so much but it blinking well does, I can tell you.

Don't matter to old Ed though because he's got other things on his mind, he's busy getting an eyeful of Welsh nurse's boobies and undoing his fly. He must've forgotten she slapped him.

—I've got a pair of tits too, I tell him, my heart slowing down again, feeling a bit softer towards him, now our Nazi argument's done with and wuzzed to nothing like a burst balloon. —I'll get them out for you if you want. Suck away like a big babby. I used to do all sorts.

But he's turned his head away and he's rummaging in his pants like there's no tomorrow, the dirty old monkey, so I'm talking to the wall.

CHICAGO BOX

Hank's all tanned, maybe it was sunny in the Abroad place. Mrs Manyon comes on all smarmy, she must fancy him.

—Oh you *are* looking well, Mr Taylor, she says. —Your mum'll be ever so thrilled to see you back, she's almost her own self again, I'm pleased to say, though at her age the memory doesn't get any better.

He's carrying this old cardboard box looks familiar. I used to have one like that in the attic way back, my Chicago box I called it. I can spot when something's wrong, his face has gone all stiff, it's fawn and sicky like a man with a bicycle on the doorstep with his cap off and a telegram in his hand saying perhaps you and your sister'd better sit down.

—She's left you, hasn't she, I go. —I always knew she would.

—What are you talking about?

—Her.

Don't like saying her name, can't get my lips round it.

—Karen?

—Well, who d'you think?

He does this noise like he wants to spit out a bad taste.

—Can't you ever give her the benefit of the doubt? I came to ask you something, he says.

—That little boy's not yours, you know. The bloke with the red car that's got eyelids, you need look no further than him.

His face goes red and he looks down, does some breathing.

—I see you've made a full recovery, he mutters.

—They can do tests now, you know, DNA tests.

—Now there's a thought, he goes, looking at me all funny peculiar.

He's stroking my Chicago box like it's a chicken he might have to slaughter, you put both hands around the neck, you twist and then you pull and it goes click. I killed a rabbit like that once too. Or wanted to. This DNA talk gives me this bad feeling but I can't put my finger on why. Don't even know what DNA is, except something in them detective dramas.

—I think we need to do some talking, Mum. About what's in here. And he taps the box.

—That box is none of your beeswax, I say. —There's nothing to talk about. Let sleeping dogs lie. All I'm saying is that Wife of yours, she's been cheating on you since the day –

—Stop, Mum! Stop that now.

He's getting up with my chicken-shaped Chicago box, which is mine, and my own private beeswax.

—Another time, Mum, when you're feeling a bit more yourself.

—But this *is* myself, how much more myself can I be? I'm the same me I've always been, so you can like it or lump it, mate!

But he's buggered off with my beeswax, doesn't even want to stay and hear a joke. I was going to tell him the one about –

I was going to tell him a joke.

*　　*　　*

—You were asking for that, says Doris. She's looking perkier than last time I saw her.

—I thought you was dead, missis, I go.

—There's dead and dead, she smiles.

—Nice lad, your son, says Ed who's come Zimmering up. He don't say hello to Doris, just stares right through her like a stranger.

—And what about you? I ask him. —Are you alive or dead?

—Feel that and you'll find out, says Ed, grabbing my hand and sticking it under the frame and between his legs. —You're a right goer, aren't you? he says, all wheezy. Old goat, he is.

—It takes one to know one, I tell him, having a bit of a feel.

Dead Doris makes a face.

Ed's thing is hard as a carrot.

There were days he could spend the night and days he couldn't. Some afternoons we'd go and watch them playing baseball on the plain, and then we'd meet the GI truck at Zetland Road and it'd take the men back to Tortworth. Those days, they were like tinned peaches and cream. Then all of a sudden Bobby was back on sick leave because he had jaundice, and Marje was hopping about like a blue-arsed fly, trying to get some leave from the factory to nurse him – which meant telling Mr Simpson she had something wrong with her ladies' bits, she was bleeding like a stuck pig, and there was even clots –

—OK, OK, you can spare us the gory details, he goes. —Take two days off and bring a sick note.

Then spending all day in bed with Bobby, the two of them at it like a couple of rabbits.

—Fixed your ladies' bits for you, has he? I go when

she finally come downstairs. —Surprised you can still walk, missis.

But she laughed.

We all went to the flicks together to see *Casablanca*, me and Ron and Marje and Bobby. Bobby said he felt happier going out in the dark cos he didn't look so yellow, being dark-haired and all he didn't want to be mistaken for a stray spic or a Jew or a Jap or nothing, and Marje laughs like a hyena even though it's not funny, what with our dad being a prisoner out in the Far East and still no news. We cried our eyes out at the flick of course and couldn't get 'As Time Goes By' out of our stupid heads, and then we all went to the Coconut Club and me and Marje got sozzled on gin and its, and the men drank beer and Ron complained like always because it wasn't cold, and the two of them started talking aeroplanes, so me and Marje got right narked cos we reckoned they loved them planes more than they loved us, they even gave them the names of women, the bomber ones anyway, and if our song hadn't started up they'd have sat there talking planes all night. But it did, and me and Ron was back in each other's arms and dancing.

> I haven't said thanks for that lovely weekend,
> Those two days of heaven you helped me to spend,
> The thrill of your kiss as you stepped off the train,
> The smile in your eyes like the sun after rain . . .

That was our song, that was.

> To mark the occasion we went out to dine,
> Remember the laughter, the music, the wine?
> The drive in the taxi when midnight had flown,
> Then breakfast next morning just we two alone . . .

Bucketloads of glamour, there was. He wasn't an American

like you see at Sea View in the afternoons, effing and blinding at each other on Jerry Springer. He wasn't trailer trash. The two of us, we were quite an eyeful. People turned to look, and we liked it. We looked *swell*.

We all walked home together through the blackout, arm in arm, and it felt like we was a family again, and I know me and Marje were both thinking how good if Mum and Dad could see us, even though Mum'd say, You have put on too much lipstick, girls, it makes you look common, and Dad'd thrash our two bums for being a couple of no-good sluts.

It was me and Ron's turn for the double bed so Marje and Bobby settled in downstairs on the settee, giggling and slapping and shrieking away, while me and Ron staggered upstairs ripping our clothes off as fast as we could, and soon the house was shaking with the four of us all at it like there was no tomorrow, because maybe there *wasn't* no tomorrow. (Everyone did in the war, don't let them tell you otherwise. If they tell you otherwise they're lying.) Oh, we couldn't keep our hands off each other, we were so full of life and he was so full of the need to grab. Even though I didn't strictly know what was what back then, I was a quick learner and he soon knew the best ways of driving me nuts and showing me how to do the stuff that drove him nuts too, and often afterwards he'd say, You sure are becoming an expert, hon, I sure trained you well. Things I'd never've dreamed of, some of them. Again and again we did it, then again in the morning till I was sore and Marjorie knocks on the door and asks if we'd like a cuppa.

And then when we've made ourselves respectable with a sheet she comes in with a nice breakfast tray and all smiling, because of getting her oats with Bobby.

—We're big girls now, she says. —Just be careful, that's all. You look after my little sister, she tells Ron, and this look swishes between them.

—I sure will, he goes, and gives me a squeeze, and Marje

sits on the end of the bed and pours the tea like we're a family, but one that flirts.

—Make sure he always uses a French letter, she tells me after. —You don't want a bun in the oven.

I'm hungry as usual. Could eat a horse. Could eat a bloody whale. The sea's flat as ironing, and we're going along the pier, me in the wheelchair, the opposite of when the baby was in the pram and me pushing and the men eyeing me up because I had a good figure with curves in all the right places and a man's eye travels easy on a curve, up and down and around like it's slippy as silk. And a man needs three things after a war. He needs a job, some beer and a woman. But sometimes just a woman'll do.

—How about one of them deckchairs, I say. —You can hire them. Then we can both sit. Have an ice lolly! D'you fancy an ice lolly, Hank? Like he's a little boy again.

—No, says Hank. —I do not fancy an ice lolly. I think it's time we talked, Mum.

—The wind's getting up.

There's something nudging away at the back of my head, but I can't put my finger on what's bothering me, I just know I need to keep a sharp lookout for what comes next.

—Now, he goes.

—It's embarrassing.

—Tell me anyway.

—Ed Mayberley made me feel his willy. Dirty old monkey.

He looks at me funny and we watch the gulls hopping about pecking at scattered chips and chicken nuggets. There's one with its toes missing, just a stump for a foot. He's walking all lopsided, trying to hop on just the one leg, but he needs to use the stump to balance.

—Look at that one. Keeps getting barged out of the way.

66

He's not long for this world, I expect. Got any new jokes for me then? I've got one, heard it from the porter. There's this couple, they have a baby but there's something wrong with it. The doctor takes them to a ward that's full of babies that's got stuff wrong with them. They stop at the first cot where there's a baby with no legs and the couple says, Is that our baby? And the doc says, No, that's not your baby. So they stop at the next cot and there's a baby with no head and they say, Oh God, is that our baby? And the doc says, No, that is not your baby, your baby is worse, I am afraid. So they stop at the next cot and there is just an eyeball on the pillow. Oh no, they say, is that our baby? Yes, says the doctor, that is your baby. But I am afraid that it is blind.

Kiddo, he don't laugh. That ain't like him, he must've heard it before.

We watch the birds some more.

—How d'you know when a Barnsley girl's had an orgasm? Eh? She drops her chips.

Still no laughing.

—Did you tell Mrs Manyon? he goes.

—About what?

—This dirty old man.

—No I ruddy well didn't.

—Why not?

—She'd be jealous, wouldn't she. She'd want some too. I said got any jokes? Your turn!

He mutters something under his breath.

—Look, Mum, I'm going to come straight out with it. What exactly happened in America? Why did we leave Chicago?

What's he talking about? I've never been to Chicago in my life. He's got this thing about America. It's all in his head.

—I could eat something. I could eat a horse all of a sudden. How about we go to the baker's, get a cake for tea?

—Tell me about you and my old man, goes Hank.

—Oh bloody hell, we've been through all this a thousand times.

—Let's go through it again.

—I remember *Food Facts* on the radio. There was this one went, *Dearly beloved brethren, is it not a sin to peel potatoes and throw away the skin?* Makes me hungry just remembering it. Know what I used to dream about? Banana custard, steak-and-kidney pie, bubble and squeak. Used to dream about which plateful I'd eat first, if I had them all in front of me at the same time.

—I'm not talking about the war, he says.

—*The skin feeds the pigs and the pigs feed us, dearly beloved brethren, is that not enough?*

—I'm talking about after the war.

—We still had rationing. It was a struggle, you've no idea. Everyone wanted to start all over again, make everything new, rebuild the country, you know. Give it a *makeover*.

—Why didn't you and my dad stay together, Mum? Why was I the only one? (Like a scratched record, he is.) —There's stuff in that box –

—Cos we didn't get on. Cos I wanted a boy and I got a boy. Didn't want no girl.

—You wanted a boy? What about my dad? What did he want?

There's this long silence, it stretches out to sea. On and on. Doris is looking at me with her new eyes.

—He didn't want nothing. No girl, no boy, no nothing.

—But I thought –

—You thought wrong.

—That box of stuff –

—They gave Doris stargazers. Make sure it's lilac when it's my turn, if it's the season. She was cremated, weren't you, D?

68

I want her on my side now.

—Tell me. His voice all choked up. Doris is looking at me. —I'd like to know the truth, please, Mum. Whatever it is. There's papers in that box –

Like a scratched record. I'm thinking: I could do with one of them Chelsea buns right now. Or a lardy-cake, or one of them Battenbergs. Or if we are talking savoury, a pork pie is what I'd go for, though it would be a toss-up between that and sausage and mash.

—Doris, she was the only one who could make sense of the *Radio Times*. There was even marzipan. Well, they called it that. It was made of beans, tasted of engine oil. I saw Churchill when he came to Bristol. I was in the crowd, and there he was, two yards away, with his bald head and his big old cigar. I cheered till I was blue in the face, waving this bunch of muddy onions I'd dug up, cos me and Marje, we had our little Victory Garden and I wanted to show the Prime Minister I was doing my bit. He was just getting back in his car when he saw me waving my onions, and our eyes met, and he winked. I swear it. Churchill winked at me cos of my Victory onions.

—Mum, goes Hank. —Stop it. Stop running your mouth and look at what I found here. Might ring a few more bells for you.

And he whips out this photo from his pocket and shoves it in my face.

—I'd like you to explain this.

Things go all quiet for a bit, because I am trying to remember what variety of onion it was, they had quite a kick to them.

—And you can tell me about Chicago too, while you're at it. And what happened to Ron, and why he never stayed in touch – because thanks to what's in here, I happen to know you've been feeding me a pack of lies from the word go. All this stuff about divorce – you never got divorced,

Mum. From him or from anyone. It's not a pleasant thing to discover, you know, that you've been lied to all your life about –

—About what? Them onions are bothering me, cos my memory's a sieve.

—Everything! Everything! About who I am!

—I haven't been lying!

—Don't make it worse, Mum. Please. I just want the truth about who my real dad is. Or was. OK?

Oh blinking heck, he's going to cry. His voice keeps wobbling about.

—Look, there's stuff in that box I don't understand, and I want to make sense of it. OK?

—None of your beeswax.

He rams the photo right in my face.

—What's that about then?

It's not my wedding photo, it's another one, of a woman and a little brat in frilly clothes, but I can't see a blasted thing without my glasses. So too bad. I shut my eyes to stop the water, them onions don't half make you cry.

—Mum, he goes, more gently.

—None of your beeswax, I say, my eyes still shut tight and now big sobs hopping up into my throat. He hands me a Kleenex and I blow and my tummy starts making gutter noises that mingle in with the seagulls.

There ain't much dignity to it.

He loved talking about beating the six kinds of crap out of the fuckin' *Luftwaffe*. He was forever on about them planes of his, he admired them probably the same way he admired my tits, as in, he could spend hours in their company, and never get bored. He loved flying, he loved them blue skies smiling at him. I got to know all about P-51 Mustangs, Spitfires, Hurricanes, Me-109s, and FW190s.

About other pilots who saved his ass, and asses he'd saved in dog-fights and bluff manoeuvres. He called the German planes pirates.

—So how do you wee up there?

—Well, we got the pee-tube, hon, he goes, stroking the tit that's nearest him.

—A pee-tube?

—Yeah, you fix it on to your dick. It's a real fuckin' hoo-ha. You gotta undo the harness, then the parachute, then the flies of your flying suit, then your underwear, get your dick out, and fish around under the seat for the pee-tube and use it while you're still in formation, still navigating, and keeping an eye out for pirates. Oh, and still flying the plane. There's quite an art to it, hon.

And he laughs, and takes a nipple in his mouth and starts sucking. Then laughing. He rolls over and snorts.

—There's this guy in the squadron, he's a bit of an inventor, he fixes up a system so he's wearing the pee-tube before he starts out. But he forgets about the altitude: it's 30 below freezing up there. So his dick starts to freeze. It's gone totally numb. So he drops altitude and gets home, spends five days in the hospital. You never saw a thing swole up so bad. Man, we laughed. But he was lucky not to lose his dick.

And then he gets back to feasting on my tits.

You couldn't help being in love with a man could tell you stuff like that. Jokes, too. We'd lie in bed and tell jokes, Polack jokes, Okie jokes, dirty jokes. Them Okies, from Oklahoma, they were hicks, he said, lived up in villages in the mountains and rolled their own, meaning did incest. So there's this boy falls in love with a girl and marries her, comes out of the bedroom on his wedding night at the family home, in shock, says, Oy, Dad! She says she's a virgin!

71

Hell, get rid of her! goes the dad. She ain't good enough for her own folks she ain't good enough for us!

I always remember a joke.

Hank's pushing me right out on to the pier. There's this smell in the air when you turn the corner on to All Saints Road, reminds me of where our mum worked before the war, the bakery.

—She just got whiter and whiter with it. Stayed in bed all day. Cancer.

—Who's that? Doris?

—No, my mum. But Doris was riddled with it too, weren't you Doris. It was a blessed release, me and Marje always said, cos war wasn't her cup of tea. Would've disrupted her routine. We were eating our lunch when we got the news about our dad. Omelettes were Marje's speciality.

—Your sister Marje? The one who died? He's bought the *Mirror,* and he's reading it.

—The hens, they'd laid one each. And we had a slice of loaf each too, no butter but a good little smear of Bovril. Me and Marje, we always called it by its short name, *Bov.* Bread and Bov and an omelette we was eating.

—Uh-huh, he goes, still reading.

—But we've barely started putting it down us when the door goes. Bit of silence between us, we've both got this sixth sense, then Marje says, Leave it Gloria, eat your omelette. Get it down you, you're skin and bone. But for once I've got no appetite.

—Uh-huh? goes Hank. He has heard this story.

—But I get up. And sure enough there's the man with his bicycle and his cap off holding the telegram, saying perhaps you and your sister had better sit down.

Hank turns the page, flattens out the paper.

—It's in that box.

—Huh? goes Hank, waking up a bit.

—Madam, we regret to inform you that Private Winstanley passed away in Changi prison camp after a short illness. He served his country with great courage, blah-di-blah. Me and Marje, we just threw our arms round each other and cried. He wasn't much of a dad but he was the only one we had.

—There's the letter from Marje, too, he goes slowly. —Can you remember what that one said, Mum?

He's looking at me funny.

—Nope. Which one was that?

—You know the one.

—There's probably some other photos of my wedding, too. My wedding dress was made of an old parachute, you know. Marje sewed it.

—I'm glad you mentioned that, he goes. —As a matter of fact there's quite a few pictures.

I said the wrong thing, didn't I.

—I'd like to talk about them.

—None of your bloody beeswax. It comes out louder than I thought.

—Why's it none of my beeswax? He's put the paper down now, and he's grabbed my hand, and he's squeezing. It hurts. —Come on, Mum! Try and remember things straight for once!

—It's gone. My memory's buggered to bits.

—Very convenient, says Doris. Look at you. Lying through your teeth!

—Well, un-bugger it! snaps Hank. He's shoved the paper down the back of the wheelchair now and he's looking at me now, all angry, still hurting my hand. —I've a right to know. I don't want to put pressure on you but –

—Talking of pressure, you are hurting my hand, plus I could do with a wee.

Can't he see I'm about to bloody blinking well cry? Don't that count for nothing?

73

—Listen. Mum. I don't want to upset you, I really don't.

—Well, don't then! Leave it be! I was a good mum to you!

—Tell him what's what! says Doris in my ear. —Stop coming out with porky pies. Just tell him the truth!

—You were a great mum, he says. —You were the best. And I know it wasn't easy bringing me up on your own. Look, I'm grateful for all that, Mum. All those sacrifices and everything, and you were never bitter or nothing. I mean it. But I still have a right to know where I came from. And I think there's someone else who has a right to know, too.

—Who's that, then?

He hands me a tissue and I blow.

—You'll find out soon enough, he says. —She's coming to pay you a visit.

And his voice, it's gone all sly. What's all that about? Who is this *she*? Shocks me because Hank, he ain't like that normally, and I can see there's more where that came from, but he stifles it, the way he always did because I'm all he's got, aren't I? *Just the two of us*, I always used to say. *Just you and me, kiddo. A boy and his mum, making their way through life and having a good old laugh.* He'd never push me and the wheelchair over the edge of the pier, however easy it was to do, cos we've got this bond, we have. He was a good baby, and a good boy, and now he's a good man, which is the one good thing I did. So he just sighs and mutters something and then takes me to use the lav in a caff because I can't hold on too long.

And in the night I remember about that marzipan, the taste of engine oil and the bean feeling of it, and the time I saw the Great Zedorro with Ron, and the time I saw him again which was after, and the price I paid for it, which was a good price or so it seemed at the time, because some things are best forgotten.

You're a swell kid.

When I wake up there's a dim memory of it all, like the shadow-shape of a thing that happened that was got rid of once and for all down the back of a sofa with a dog lying asleep on it, all peaceful and snuffling in its dreams. *You're a swell kid, hon. You're a swell kid.*

NO IRISH NO DOGS NO JEHOVAH'S WITNESSES

And now that you're gone, dear, this letter I pen,
My heart travels with you till we meet again.
Keep smiling, my darling, and sometime we'll spend
A lifetime as sweet as that lovely weekend.

For a man who can't hold a tune he likes to sing, my
blue-eyed airman, but do I care? No, cos I'm head over
heels in love, I am. He's been singing away, bits of this
and bits of that, and I must've dozed off to the buzz of his
voice, and when I wake up his chest's moving differently,
and the noise isn't singing, it's crying.
—What's the matter?
I'm wiping at his tears and hugging him and kissing him
all at once, because seeing a big brave man cry is a horrible
sight. No one wants to see that, it does you in.
—I'm scared the whole fuckin' time, man.
—Silly sausage. Course you are. Nothing to be ashamed
of. You'd be mad not to be scared.
—Few times, I'm up there, I find myself whispering, God,
you gotta. You gotta get me back. God, listen, you gotta.
—Do you believe in Him?
—Nope.
—It'd help.
—Well, it don't stop me praying. Some of the guys,

they'll promise God they'll swear off liquor and women, if he'll pull them through.

I reach down to the floor for my knickers, and wipe his tears with a corner of them.

—Don't you swear off me.

—Don't worry, hon. I figure if God's really God, he'd understand how men feel about women. He smiles. —And liquor. And a whole lotta stuff.

And so I sing to him. I ain't got much of a voice neither, but it cheers him up.

> Underneath the spreading chestnut tree,
> I loved her and she loved me.
> Now you ought to see our family
> 'Neath the spreading chestnut tree . . .

I must've slept, because when I open my eyes I get the shock of my life: it's Hank standing there with Marje.

—Marje! Bloody hell, I go. You might've warned me, turning up like that.

—Not Marje, Mum, he says. —This lady's name is Jill. She's been wanting to meet you.

Lady? Jill? I don't know no ladies and I don't know no Jills. But I know a Marje when I see one. I blink. I need my specs. When I've got them on I have another look and I am right flummoxed, and not sure for a minute where I am or when I am. She's got Marje's mouth that's Mum's mouth too. She's nervous but trying to hide it, twisting at her scarf. The scarf is bluey-green with peacock feathers, the type that costs.

—How much was it then?

—Sorry? she goes.

—That scarf, how much it set you back?

She looks at Hank.

—Er, it's Liberty, she goes. —About thirty pounds?

—You mean you can't remember?

—No. Well, not exactly.

—Mum, goes Hank. —I said this is Jill.

She's not exactly at ease, this Jill who isn't Marje, but has her mouth, and Mum's, and can't remember how much she paid for a scarf. In fact I get the feeling she's right nervous. Her eyes, they're flitty. She's in her fifties, maybe sixty. What's she –

Oho, I get it! Oh, oh, oh!

And there is a big wash of relief that's almost as good as letting go of a big wee, cos I've realised who she is. I am a dumb one, I am! Of course of course of course, she is Hank's girlfriend! Ho ho, I didn't know you were allowed to keep women on oil rigs! Not that I don't approve. I always thought Hank could do better than Karen, and I'm not the only one, that shop of hers is a front for something, you can bet, and she's a crap mum too. You can't spend the amount of time she does having leg waxes and be a good one, can you.

—That's my boy, Hank, I go, patting his knee. —Good for you! That's more like it! Give that Wife of yours a taste of her own medicine!

—Gloria, goes the woman called Jill. —I've been want-ing to meet you for –

She stops and does this big gulp.

—All my life I've felt something was missing, a part of me wasn't there. And – well. I'm so glad we – well, as I said, I've been wanting to meet you for years.

Years, eh? She's a passionate one. And Hank's a dark horse and all.

When I was in hospital, there was this demolition site you could see from the window. One day an orange crane came, and began swinging this wrecking ball. Smashing down the walls of what used to be Woolworth's, and some flats.

79

It was good to watch that wrecking ball. Wrecking and wrecking.

But some things isn't wrecked the same way as houses, some things takes a slower time and does it more invisible, like an apple rotting. And some things is wrecked with too much squeezing, like a hand grabbing your bare heart. And fish is killed in the sea sometimes with underwater explosions which shocks them to death.

So there are lots of ways you can wreck stuff, see.

Not so many ways to mend them though. Not when they're that wrecked.

—Mrs Taylor, goes the lady called Jill, and her hand's shaking with nerves, she's reaching it out to me shaking shaking, I don't know what I'm supposed to do with it so I sort of clutch it and then let it drop. —Can I call you Gloria?

She's not a bad looker, but way too old for him of course, and posh, because there's a camel coat like the visitors Noreen gets, the Lady Muck type, but I can tell she's nervous.

—And my name's Jill Farraday, she says.

—Farraday? I go, because unlike Zedorro the name doesn't ring any sort of bell. —Do I know you?

—You knew me once, she says. —A long time ago.

—How come you've got the jitters? I go. —You seen a ghost?

But I like the feeling of power, that was what was missing with Hank's Wife, she didn't have the respect.

—Never mind that you're a bit old for him, I go, he's better off with a mature woman. But I hope you're not a clever one, cos clever don't suit him, just look at the shape of his head, it's a good shape but he's no brain-box, none of us are.

—Karen's waiting in the other day room, goes Hank.

Now I'm confused.

—So she knows? She knows about this one?

—Yes, goes Hank. —They've met.

—It's not what you think, says the Lady Muck woman who's called Jill, looking at me funny. —I'm not his girlfriend. You must realise that. I wrote you a letter once. And I sent a photo with it. Can you – remember that?

—When?

—Oh, years ago, she says.

—Well then.

Silence.

—I thought you might –

—Might what?

—Never mind. It doesn't matter.

—Yes it does, says Hank. He's looking as grim as a bloody undertaker, he is.

And she's looking ill, it seems to me. Pale as a blob of putty.

—There's a bowl you can use for sick, I tell her. —Even a commode if you want one.

—Yes, she says, looking round. —They've thought of everything then, it's a nice place.

—Nice? It's full of foreigners. The staff, they're all black or brown except for a couple. The new one, she's yellowish, but she can't even speak English.

There's a bit of silence while she looks even sicker and Hank goes red and looks down.

—It's . . . good to meet you at last, says the woman.

—Yes, I go, because I don't know what else to say.
—Well, who the hell are you then?

They give each other a look.

—Well, she goes slowly. —You used to know me. When I was very young.

—How young?

—Just a baby.

—So who's your mum? Did I know your mum? Are you Iris's sister's daughter? Are you Mrs O'Malley's little girl?

She just looks at me.

—I was hoping you might remember me, she says, and her face goes all tilted.

—Well, I'd like to, dear, I tell her. Though it is not strictly the truth, I couldn't give a flying watchermacallit.

Hank's about to say something, he's bursting to say it, but she stops him.

—Please, she goes, and puts up her hand. —We agreed.

Her voice has gone croaky. There's this look passes between them like they've had a lovers' tiff.

—This isn't going to be easy for either of us, Gloria. But – well. It needs to be done, and it's taken me a lifetime to get this far and –

—A lifetime? How old are you then?

—And there are things I need to know, that will help me feel complete. Do you understand what I'm saying, Gloria? There are things I need to know, and that means there are things you need to try and remember.

—Tall order for someone what's got Mad Cow, I go.

—Well. I'm prepared to be very patient, she says. —But for now I think . . . I think I'll leave you, and come back another time. And she's snapping her handbag shut like a mouth. —I need to collect my thoughts, I think. This has been quite – well. Quite an ordeal, really.

—Mum, can't you – begins Hank, but she stops him again.

—Please don't, she says. —She'll remember when she's ready.

—*If*, he says, looking daggers at me. —*If* she's ready. Personally, I have a feeling she might never be. All due respect, Jill, you don't know her like I do.

Why is he treating me so rude and cruel? He is a good boy!

—We discussed this, Hank. I'm fine. Really. Look, I'm going to write my name down for you, Gloria, she says, scrabbling about with a bit of paper. —It might . . . jog your memory. And her face twists into a shape. JILL FARRADAY, she writes. —And my birthday too, why not? And she scribbles some numbers. —I was born at the end of the war, she says, looking at me sideways. —The same day it ended.

Well, bully for you, I'm thinking, but I try and make my mouth do a smiling thing.

—The kind of date you'd remember, isn't it? she goes. —If you lived through the war?

—Might be, might not. Bit of a blank to me, I go.

—Oh. Well, perhaps it will . . . come back to you, she says, looking pissed off. —Anyway – goodbye . . . *Gloria*.

And she holds out her hand, wanting another shake. I give it a pat and I say —Goodbye, dear, like a nice old lady, and then she suddenly rams her face down at me and kisses my cheek and then with a flurry she and her expensive scarf go stumbling away.

—What's that all about then, I go. —She's only just arrived and she's buggered off.

—You really don't know, do you, Mum? he goes. —Remember that box of stuff? Full of your old paper-work? Remember the photo I showed you? You really haven't guessed? Mum? Mum?

—Well, who do you think I am, a bloody mind-reader? Hank gets up to leave.

—Well, who is she then?

He sighs.

—I'd tell you, Mum, I really would. But she wants you to remember for yourself, he says, walking out.

—Well, don't we all! What a bloody nerve! D'you think I enjoy having a memory like a sieve? I call after him – but not as loud as I'd like to, cos the little drowned girl behind the curtain, she's all full of hate again, I can feel it, hate that's full of mud and dripping with pond-weed. So as soon as I see Hank's car drive off I go over to where Ed's asleep in his wheelchair and put my hand on his stinkhorn thingummybob and start stroking away.

> Underneath the spreading chestnut tree,
> I loved her and she loved me.
> Now you ought to see our family
> 'Neath the spreading chestnut tree . . .

I ain't much of a singer, but the singing and the stroking Ed's old thingummy, it calms me down, it does, I could do it all day.

> She said I love you,
> And there ain't no ifs or buts.
> He said I love you,
> And the crowd all shouted –

And then right on cue, Ed wakes up and yells the last bit with me:

CHESTNUTS!

—Chestnuts, Gloria!

He sighs, cos he's died and gone to heaven of course, with a woman attending to his whatsit, bless him. But nothing much happens to be honest which is a bit of a disappointment, and he don't smell of roses neither. He leans back in his wheelchair, eyes shut.

—Oh Gloria, he says. —I knew you liked me.

Well, it's nothing to do with like, is it. But we could use some baby oil, I'm thinking.

—Oh Gloria. Glorious Gloria, heh heh, he goes, then starts humming. *Underneath the spreading chestnut tree . . .*

—There was this famous hypnotist, I'm telling him, he used to do a show in the Little Theatre off Whiteladies Road, me and Ron went to see him. He was the cat's pyjamas, he was, he was in ENSA, he travelled all over the country doing shows for the troops and up in London, but he came from Bristol. Ever so young but he knew his stuff, he made this woman lie on a chair, balance a bowl of oranges on her belly, I saw it with my own eyes, I've got a picture of her somewhere from the local paper. Then other times I heard he'd get the whole audience lifting their hands up when a tune played. Marje went once and he made everyone feel you were freezing cold in the middle of summer. Wonder what happened to him.

—Well, if he was still alive I could use his services, says Ed, and he pats my hand that's rubbing away at his whatsit to make sure I've got his gist.

—I don't think he stretched to that, I go, and all of a sudden my heart isn't in it any more and I slow down on his thing. —Shall we ask Mrs M for a cup of tea instead? I'm that parched.

I used to like what I could do to men, I used to like that double-glazed look that came in their eyes when I was giving them the pleasure, and how grateful they were after and how I'd sometimes get an extra half-crown from the generous ones like Mr Loomis. Look at me now doing it for free.

—What's that? says Ed.

—For free! I yell in his ear that's not deaf. —I'm doing it for free!

When I wake up I turn on the telly, which is another of them makeover programmes, there's this woman wants everything green because she's always been interested in plants and biology and the jungle in particular though she's never actually been there, it's her passion, she says, it's the theme of her life.

—Out with the old, in with the new, says the designer. He has one of those squishy bottoms that looks like a girl's.

—That's what you need, Gloria, says Mrs Manyon, after being ill.

—Leather trousers?

—No, a bit of a makeover. Want me to get the hairdresser to come in so you can be all spruced up for your visit?

—What visit, I go, and then I remember about that bloody woman coming back like a bad penny. I can't shake her off, you'd have thought with her money she had better things to do, she could go to John Lewis with her chequebook and come away with a whole set of Wedgwood.

—You should have one of them signs like in pubs, no dogs no Irish, I tell Mrs Manyon, because Farraday's an Irish name, I reckon, unlike Zedorro. Anyway I'm too old for a makeover.

—Well, let's just give you a nice wash then. Bit of perfume, powder your nose.

Ed's looking at me.

—You was probably a good-looking woman once, he says. —I'd have fancied you. I'd have shown you a good time. Still might.

—You should be so lucky.

But it ain't strictly the truth. You'll make do with any old bit of groping at my age, it's not like you think, you still need to feel certain things in that department if you get my meaning. I might ask him if he wants to go all the way. If he can make a carrot of himself again, he could stick it in my whatsit. See if he keels over.

I used to be a *swell kid*.

*   *   *

It's three weeks after Bobby's gone away again after his jaundice, and Ron's just been transferred to Manston, so me and Marje we're a couple of wallflowers again, and bickering a bit, because of not getting sexually seen to. At the factory Marje got into big trouble with Mr Simpson for lying about her ladies' bits and not having no doctor's note, so it is a bad time. It's a Wednesday, and I've finished my shift and I'm looking out for Marje at the factory gate to have a quick hello when she comes in. But she don't turn up.

I wait and wait.

Maybe I've missed her, I think, maybe she came early – so I go back in. The others've got in overalls and started, but her overalls and her turban they're still hanging on the hook.

And that's when I think: oh shit, oh buggering broomsticks.

I've got this sixth sense, always have, so I don't even bother telling Mr Simpson, I just hurtle out of there like a bat out of hell and run all the way home.

And sure enough something has gone wrong. Something has turned horrible. You can hear her screaming from halfway down the street. The upstairs window's open but the front door's shut and there's a little huddle of neighbours on the step including Moira from number 15 blubbing her eyes out and panicking.

—She won't let us in, she gabbles.

So I fish out my key and barge in and there she is up in Mum and Dad's room, crouched on the floor clutching the parachute, that's now halfway to being a dress, flaps of paper and pins all over it. She's holding it to her belly and snotting all over it.

She don't need to say nothing. I put my arm round the poor ninny and she shakes me off and wails. But after a while she lets me hold her close and we sit there rocking and rocking.

I was right, she shouldn't've started making that dress. Bad luck, wasn't it?

That night Bobby's family get drunk as skunks and there's this big wake round at Redland, but with no body to cry over, and me and Marje shriek and snivel along with the rest of them, and get shocking plastered, and Bobby's mum says she will never laugh again as long as she lives, she lost her bestest boy, and Marje says she lost the only man in the whole world she will ever love, and we all look at the photo album of Bobby what shows his life from when he was a chubby toddler eating sand on the beach to a boy in short trousers with a prize conker and then a dark pirate man with black eyes and a hot smile, the one that swept Marje off her feet and then got ditched but came back for more, and now is scattered in pieces over Munich.

Next morning I'm there when a letter comes from him, like a warning, or a bad joke. Bobby was fond of pranks and you can't help wondering. Good thing it's me sees the postman, he gives me the letter and I put two and two together and stuff it straight in the pocket of my pinny. But too late for my eagle-eyed sis, hangover or no hangover.

—What's that? she goes, face all bleary, she looks a sight, her hair all over the place. Three out of ten is all you'd give her today and her poise has upped and died.

—Nothing. A letter from Ron, from Manston. Might be temporary, might not, and he can't tell me no more cos you've got to Be Like Dad, Keep Mum.

—Ron doesn't write letters, says Marje. —He ain't the type.

—He is now.

—Show me.

Her eyes is red and all puffy from the crying. Her nose

too, and she must've bitten her lower lip because it's all swollen up. It still looks like Mum's mouth but a joke of it, like someone's taken the mickey.

—It won't help, I say.

—Show it me.

I cover up the pocket of my pinny but she lunges out and grabs my hand – scratches me – and she's fished it out and seen right away it's from Bobby.

—He's not dead, see!

She's screaming with excitement, jumping up and down.

—They got it wrong, he's written me a letter, look! See the postmark? This was sent from Portsmouth on . . .

She stops, all puzzled and confused.

—I'll have to check the other postmark, she says. —The one on the captain's letter.

And she smiles this huge smile.

—See, it was just one of them mistakes, she says, ripping open the letter. —He's writing to tell me he's alive, and it was a mistake. The captain made a mistake.

She holds it out so we can both read, but my eyes is too blurry after a minute.

Dear darling Marje,

Tonight we are going on another mission, so I just wanted to write to you before I go to thank you for being the sweetest, most adorable, most beautiful, sexy girl there ever was . . .

But she can't read no more, can she.

THE BIG SMOKE

I have this dream but when I wake up, it's still going on. The Jill woman, she's sat by my chair talking to a slutty girl who is chewing gum and painting her toenails red.

—This is my dad and my mum in the hospital where Dad worked, she says. She must be showing her a photo, I could see it too if I wasn't pretending to be asleep. I bet they are a posh nice-looking couple, wearing tweed. Typical war people, honest folk doing their bit for England, in this case working in a hospital.

—I wasn't born at that stage, she tells the girl. —All the pictures after that, all the ones with me in, they don't look nearly so happy. Maybe that's why I always felt something was missing.

She don't half feel sorry for herself, that one. Get on with your blinking life, missis, I feel like yelling at her. There's people would kill for the kind of money you've got, just look at them clothes, just look at the luck you must've had.

—Always wanted a brother or a sister but – well, they couldn't, or they wouldn't. He'd bring his patients home sometimes, the successful ones. The others just stayed in the hospital, I suppose, or went home to their families, if their families could cope. There was one called Ned, he was young but he had white hair. Dad had helped him in the war, he'd had amnesia and then when Dad had helped him get his memory back, he couldn't cope and he went crazy. Dad treated him for years, he was part of our family. Sometimes he'd get these attacks, and Dad would have to calm him down. They'd go into the study together and maybe Dad gave him a shot or something, and then you'd hear him talking, calming him down, saying soothing things. It always worked. I think my father was probably a genius.

Funny the dreams you have.

I'm waving like billy-o in the April sunshine, waving till my arm near drops off and the train shunts out of Temple Meads and drags Marje away further and further till it's just a black dot. Oh me oh my, I'll miss her like mad, I will, even miss her wretched grief which has lasted two weeks now, and no letting up. She's left munitions to drive ambulances and she's needed in London, so I'm to take in a family that's arriving any time now, like it or lump it, raids or no raids, hard cheese and tough titty. Going back down Whiteladies Road there's tears running down my cheeks, for Bobby, for Marje, and for me, because Ron's still at Manston, and I might never see him again neither, them pilots gets shot down the whole bloody time, men like Bobby and Ron are dropping like flies, just random-like, one day he is alive and seeing to Marje's ladies' bits and the next he don't exist no more, all because of a war that no one asked for. Which is why something inside me is singing a sad bitsy little song with no real tune that goes, *Nothing'll be the same, nothing and never.*

And you know things are bad when even the goodbye present your sis gave you, a pair of utility stockings that cost three and six, can't cheer you up.

They're waiting on the doorstep for me, a bunch of brats and a fat woman name of Mrs O'Malley with a face like thunder. Irish they are, bombed out from the slums.

—They told me two bedrooms, she says. —This is just a little terrace house. I'll be back to the billeting officer right away, I will. This won't do us, d'you see how many littlies I got here?

Four or five, I reckon, mooching shoulders and dirty faces all of them.

—It's my house, I go. —And please yourself, I didn't want no lodgers anyway.

That is the start of our own little war, between her and me, I am Churchill and she is Hitler.

I don't despise bog-trotters but don't get me wrong I don't like them either, you're supposed to be big-hearted and maybe I'm not but can you blame me being miserable, Marje off to learn ambulance-driving, saying she's got to do more for her country as if risking your arm like Iris every day isn't doing something, I should coco. Very first morning and Mrs O Malley's out collecting my hens' eggs without so much as a by your leave, you'd have thought all those months kipping in shelters they might be above stealing, but oh no. This bunch of bog-trotters by the way is just one teeny fraction of the O'Malley Family. A couple of men are in a convalescent place and two other lads are off 'after getting themselves kilt', and for all I know there is squillions of cousins just queuing up to join them in my house.

You can bet we're getting sick of this ruddy war by now. And it don't get no better neither, because the billeting officer says, You get what you're given, ladies. Don't you know there's a war on?

So life goes on, the big war outside and the little war at home, all about territory and invasion by foreigners, in between my twelve-hour shifts. Then one day a small thing

93

happens that gets big later. I'm still in munitions but on Saturdays when we knock off early I've got this sideline boiling up soap, children from everywhere, the same gang that collects your jam jars, they bring me the old bits of soap and I make new cakes of it in little dishes. I've been at the grocer's delivering my cakes of soap and I'm on the way home with my fresh loaf, and I see this man walking out of the bank, looks ever so familiar. His moustache has gone and his hair's a shade lighter and he's dressed in normal civvie clothes and not his black and scarlet cape, so it takes me a moment to clock who it is. And when I do, I get such a queer feeling I can hardly credit it.

I am winded, I am, seeing him like that after last being in his company as a human rod of iron. And this thing comes over me, says, *Get yourself a better look, Gloria, make sure it's really him*, so I cross the street.

Why not follow. It's curiosity, I suppose, about the moustache being gone and the hair being different, and him looking so ordinary, like a bank clerk – not even foreign-looking any more, and being here in Bristol and not touring with ENSA wowing the troops like I heard he was doing. He goes down Percy Street and then turns left into Adelaide Road, then right into Leavesden Avenue and into a house. Number 47. You can see him through the window of his living-room. A nice ordinary living-room, with pictures on the walls and a woman who stands up from where she's been sitting sewing, and goes over and kisses him. I can only see the back of her head but I know straightaway who she is. She's the Slut Fairy.

And d'you know what? I feel this jealousy something terrible cos I'm seeing my future and realising it ain't like theirs, it ain't as happy. A life like they've got, the Great Zedorro and the Slut Fairy, a nice life at number 47 Leavesden Avenue –

There's this little voice saying, *A life like that, it's not going to be for you, Gloria, is it? Is it, my girl?*

Hank's off on the rigs again, but the new girlfriend, the older-woman one, she's very persistent about getting into my good books. I'm beginning to think she's trying to sell me something, God or a policy or something about family trees that we was always getting through the door when I lived with Hank and Hank's Wife.

The little girl's still behind the curtain but whenever this woman Jill's there she goes all shy, won't come out, won't even twitch. So maybe it is God or a church thing.

—But I don't have a family tree, I tell her, we're not even big enough to be a shrub. My cousin Joe's son got himself killed in the Falklands, and don't get me talking about Marje. We're a family of orphans. Just me and Hank. Anyway we're from Bristol. Well, London in fact, Cheapside, cos Dad was in meat. Then we moved to Bristol and he worked the buses.

—Bristol? Her face lights up like she's been there and likes it.

She's holding my hand but I'm not sure it appeals to me much. You can tell she's rich cos her rings ain't fakes. She is a lady.

—Are you a Jehovah's Witness, I go. —I mean like an undercover one?

She looks across at Mrs M then, and Mrs M makes a face.

—So why did you move from Bristol?

—Fresh start, I suppose, after the baby was born. Anyway I was always a Londoner. In Bristol they used to call me and Marje the Cockneys.

She pretends there's a wrinkle in her skirt that needs smoothing.

—A fresh start?

—Bit of a makeover, you know, out with the old, in with the new, leather trousers and all that. I can't remember that far back, to be honest. Hank's Wife says I've got that Mad Cow thing. He's better off with you, believe me.

—It's not like that, she says. —Hank and I are – friends.

—You're more than friends, I go. I sort of snap it, I don't know why, and she looks at me all funny.

—Well, you tell me, she says slowly. —You never replied to my letter. Maybe now –

What letter? I'm thinking.

—Go on, says dead Doris.

—I can't. Sorry.

—Why not? She's gripping my hand now, and you'd think she was going to cry but it's anger in fact and I wonder if I'm heading for a slap. Chilly voice. —Hank says there's nothing major wrong with your memory, the doctor says it too. He says the short-term's affected by a spot of dementia after your stroke but the long-term is fairly intact. That's what he told me.

—Well, memory's a funny thing, ain't it. It don't always work the way you think, you ask the Great Zedorro.

—The Great Zedorro? she goes. —Who's he?

—He hypnotised me once.

—Where?

—In Bristol. Ron took me to see him. He put a bowl of oranges on my tummy. I was a human rod of iron and they cheered like mad. My picture was in the paper, I've got it somewhere. You want to see it? Me and him and the Slut Fairy.

—You said you left Bristol after the baby was born, she goes. —Which baby was that?

Is she stark raving bonkers?

—Well, Hank of course, I only had the one, didn't I. And I had my hands full with him, all on my own.

She does this gulp.

96

—Two, she says. —Actually.

—Pardon? Two actually what?

—I said two. You had two. Actually. Two babies, Gloria.

She looks even more like Marje when her mouth goes down at the sides like that.

There's this long pause, and I watch the gulls outside, thinking: *two babies?*

—You've got yourself in a muddle, dear.

She doesn't like that idea. Look at her, twisting up her pretty scarf. There's another of these long silences, we're getting good at them. Then whoosh, something's blown a gasket cos she's stood up and knocked the chair over.

—You're doing it on purpose! Hank warned me about this! Admit it! There's nothing wrong with your memory, you just don't want to think about it, do you?

Not as ladylike as she looks, is she? She has one hundred per cent lost it here, if she was a child of mine I would thrash her bum.

—Think about what? I go, because I genuinely have no frigging idea, do I, and it is beginning to seem a bit laughable.

—About me! How can you just sit there and – pretend you've forgotten who I am!

What's she on about? A woman turns up. Knows Hank. Might be his mistress, if he's taken to older women. Might be a religious type, you can never tell. Might even –

Uh-oh. Now I've got it! This big laugh comes out, I can't help it.

She thinks I'm her blinking mum!

—But I don't *have* a daughter! I tell her. I'm still laughing.

—You're the one who said daughter, she says slowly, shaking. —Not me.

—Someone's been leading you up the garden path, love.

97

I never wanted a daughter! A daughter's the last thing I wanted!

I'm still laughing, which don't make her no happier. I'm laughing so loud that old Ed starts playing with himself in his sleep, and Mrs Manyon comes up looking like the grim reaper. But before anyone can say something to calm her down, which is what's needed, the Jill woman's stormed out of the day room like a bloody kid. Crying! Has she lost it or what?

That's when I know she's not a Jehovah's Witness. She's just an ordinary impostor like the fish at Gadderton Lake.

Mrs Manyon's watching her go, all puffed-up and full of outrage. And even though I can't see it on her face, I know that Doris thinks I'm in the wrong as well.

So I've got the whole ruddy world against me now. I try to remember a joke a man told me, it had a mushroom in it, a mushroom that goes into a bar. But the punchline's disappeared, and when I wake up it's dark and I'm the only one there and my face is wet like I've been rained on in my sleep like garden furniture and there is a man on TV talking about black holes in space.

Iris comes to visit us at the factory, with her missing arm, which is in fact a missing arm and shoulder. Meaning that, instead of looking like a woman, she looks like three-quarters of one.

—We are honoured, goes Mr Simpson, to welcome Iris today, and I think we can all agree she is a very brave girl to come back here and urge you to carry on the good work, because the war effort's more important than it ever was, eh, Iris?

But Iris is a ghost, she is. All she does is swing round slowly like she's on castors. She nods her head but you can see she don't recognise none of us, in our turbans.

Even out of them I'd bet she couldn't, look at her, her face is like a lump of uncooked bread-dough someone's chucked against the wall, sagging its way down. Not the person she was, not even three-quarters of the person she was. More like a quarter. We all go very quiet and then someone drops a lid that clangs and she nearly jumps out of her skin. Maisie Fielding starts to giggle, and there's some coughing and then at last – it feels like a year goes by – Mr Simpson has the nous to start clapping and we all clap and clap and clap like fury, as if we could clap her out of there, clap her up into the air and out of the window, and she just stands there with her coat-sleeve hanging loose and her shoulder gone like a big chunk out of a rectangular block of cheddar, and the tears starts pouring down her face and Mr Simpson says, Thank you, ladies, thank you, Iris, and leads her very gently away.

What war does to you is this. If you are a woman you are not out there having a crack at Jerry, are you. You are in a factory like Iris or driving ambulances or making tea in shelters or working as a land girl pulling up frozen beets with bare hands, and you are waiting to hear that your man's been killed, and getting the comfort of a little peach syrup once in a while, to make up for the youth you've lost and the coffee that's made of Spam and acorns and dead rats. And if you have a boyfriend who is a GI when D-Day comes along, watch out for some heartbreak cos he might never come back, and realising that, it'll be like one of them pilotless flying bombs when the rocket motor cuts out and it starts falling in slow motion to hit some poor bastard, no ack-ack to warn them, no nothing, because the thing's a robot, don't have no human heart guiding it down, don't have no rhyme or reason to the violence and where it hits. It's just random, and random things is worse than stuff that's planned.

*　　　*　　　*

At last I get a weekend in the Big Smoke, that I haven't been back to since I was a kid. A whole two days to escape Mrs O'Malley's blathershite and the factory and the soap-boiling, and trekking out to Yatton to buy potatoes: a night to see Marje and then the next night, if he can swing it, a night with Ron. Marje is still crying herself to sleep every night, she says in her letters, even though Ron takes her out when he gets R and R, to cheer her up. They've been to the Scala a few times, had dinner in an Italian restaurant once with her flatmate and some pals. But most of the time she just drives her ambulance and cries, because she keeps thinking she sees Bobby.

Yesterday was terrible. And I was so sure it was him! He was crossing Ardle Street and as soon as I saw him, I didn't hesitate, I swerved and followed him, driving down the wrong side of the road. I swear, Gloria, I nearly ran him down! But it wasn't him of course, it was some other man who went foul-mouthed on me, cursing and yelling, and I stalled the ambulance and so I was stuck there with him bawling me out. A whole crowd gathered. I was so embarrassed. I completely lost my poise.

Her flatmate Helen's away visiting her parents: there's a coke fire and wet clothes hanging up to dry above it, getting blackened from the soot, and a table all jumbled up with teapots and newspaper and –
—Been going out with a Yank then? I go.
—What? she says, like I've slapped her.
—Them Lucky Strikes.
She laughs, all flustered, and picks up the packet from the table.
—Oh they're Helen's. She's got a GI. I can't believe some of these American names! He's called Chuck, this bloke. But she's had a Buddy and a Leeroy too. He was black.

—Who?

—Leeroy. The white GIs and the black ones, they don't mix. They hate each other. You know what Buddy did when he heard Helen had been out with Leeroy?

—What?

—He dumped her.

—Why?

—Cos he was black. He made her promise she hadn't slept with Leeroy.

—And had she?

—Course she bloody well had. And he knew it, so he dumped her. She's got a Canadian on the side, so she's well stocked with Viceroy. Shall we nick a pack? She won't mind, she's not really a smoker, she just collects them. Or d'you prefer the Luckies?

She is in a right state of fidgetyness, she is.

Smoke smoke smoke that cigarette . . . she sings, lighting hers and then mine. She's trying to be cheerful, but her voice is all cracked with the strain of it.

Puff puff puff and if you smoke yourself to death,
Tell Saint Peter at the Golden Gate that you hates to make
   him wait,
You gotta have another cigarette . . .

It's Tex Williams.

We sit there smoking and drinking tea, the blackened clothes dripping into the bath in the next room, singing verses of 'Smoke Smoke Smoke' and arguing about the words to it because we can't remember them all.

—Let's go out tonight, says Marje. —Go to one of them Bottle Clubs. You bring them stockings I gave you?

—No.

I don't tell her this, but I'm saving them for my wedding.

—OK, you paint my legs, I'll paint yours.

So we dress up and swab our legs with old tea that Marje keeps in a special pot, and do the line on each other's legs with brown ink, except mine's wobbly, it keeps getting snafued and Marje gets cross and washes it off and makes me start again.

We end up in Half Moon Street, jitterbugging with GIs, and putting back the gin and limes and them with their bourbons. We're soon a bit blotto. We're swaying in the corner between dances when two GIs come up to us. They're each holding out one stocking.

—You want the other, gals? says one.

I don't know what he's on about until Marje slaps his face.

—Oversexed, overpaid and over here! she snaps, and storms off. —Come on, Gloria, let's get out of here! She's quicker on the uptake, being the clever one.

I follow, but as soon as we're on the street the Moaning Minnie goes off.

—If it's got our name on it, says Marje, still stomping along all angry on her platforms.

—No, let's go in somewhere, I go.

The stocking thing, it's left a bad taste, and I don't want that to end the evening. So we duck into this little downstairs pub on Windmill Street. It's so smoky you can't see a thing to begin with, and the music's loud. But then we get used to it, and I look at Marje, and Marje looks at me, and we make a face and burst out laughing, cos we can't believe our luck. These are the best-looking bloody Yanks you've ever seen. And we're almost the only women in the room. Just us and the bar-girl.

—Now we're talking, I yell in M's ear over the noise, but already I'm noticing there's something funny about this place, because none of them hardly looks at us. Not what we're used to, two blonde good-lookers like us, though one is twenty per cent better-looking than the other, which is me.

—Let's put on that new lipstick of yours, I go to Marje, thinking a touch of red'll do the trick. —Find the Ladies.

We squeeze through, and come out to some steps.

—Got it on the black market, Marje says, pulling out the lipstick from her handbag. —Bloke says it's made of some kind of lubrication stuff they use in tractor engines.

—Yum yum, I say, hope we don't get blisters, and am about to tell her this joke I heard one of Mrs O'Malley's brats telling, about a talking horse, when I stop and grab her arm.

—My God! she whispers. Cos she has seen it too.

Two full-sized, hulking grown men in uniform, standing on the steps –

Snogging.

Locked together, they are, kissing each other's bloody faces off. One has his hand in the other one's hair, his big hairy hand that has a wedding ring on the finger. It's like their mouths is glued together.

Bloody hell. So we just stand there for a bit, till Marje gets the giggles and we have to run out screaming our heads off with laughter.

—Fairies! she's shrieking. —It's a fairy club!

Outside we stumble our way through the blackout, and you can hear the bombs falling.

—There's these two fairies, I tell her. —They're setting up house together. (I've just remembered this joke, Maisie at the factory told it me.) —And there's one up a step-ladder, and he's hanging up pictures on the walls and the other one's helping, and the one on the ladder, he does a little fart. And the other fairy goes, Oh, why talk of love when there's work to be done?

Marje laughs a bit, but not much. The fairies, they're bothering her.

—Fighting men shouldn't be fairies, she says. —Grown-up, good-looking men like that. Bloody hell, they were in uniform! Men's uniform! Don't they know there's a war on?

We walk on a bit more and she tells me about her Wren friend who says there's a lot of lesbians there and the WVS is riddled with them, she's seen girls snogging too, and squishing each other's tits, and soon we're cheered up and singing the chorus of 'Smoke Smoke Smoke' again, because it's the only bit we can agree on. When we're worn out from that, we go along in silence for a while, arm in arm, stumbling around the bomb-craters in our silly shoes.

The darkness makes it easier to talk, and there's stuff I want to ask her but she's so twitchy, it's like walking on eggs. But finally I do it.

—What'll you do, Marje? I mean, you've been going out. I mean like tonight – I know it wasn't much, but it's not the first time, is it? So there's going to come a time when you can imagine life without – you know.

I don't say the name Bobby, it might set her off, so I just leave it hanging, and she don't reply. There's this long silence, and I'm beginning to wonder if she's so blotto she didn't hear a word I said.

—You've got to grab love with both hands when it comes along, Gloria, she says finally, her voice all slurry with the booze, passing me the fag. —I don't think you understand that. You might be my sister but let's face it you're none too bright.

—So you're always telling me, I go, a bit stung. —But I'm bright enough to be following your advice this time.

—How's that?

—Cos that's what I'm doing with Ron. I'm grabbing and I'm holding on.

But then I feel sorry for her again cos I think: how must

that make her feel, with bits of Bobby scattered all over Munich?

But it don't seem to register.

—Grab it with both hands, she says, and hold on to it. No matter what.

And I can feel the tightness in her arm that's linked to mine, and feel these shudders running through her which must be to stop herself from crying, and I think how lucky I am to be seeing Ron tomorrow.

I thought it would be easy with him, but it wasn't. He'd changed, war changes you, it's stupid to think it don't. Drink changes you too.

He'd already had a few by the time he turned up, you could tell from his walk – that same cocky walk but with a swagger to it that he wasn't all in control of. I felt this squeeze of love when I saw him in his uniform, a big squeeze on my heart like the first time he stood on our doorstep, before we went to see the Great Zedorro. I felt faint with it, and then I felt I was melting away in the heat of him, and it was to do with him being a GI too, a pilot who risked his life for us and might still die, which made me feel ill. And feel like giving him everything. Whatever he wanted from me I would give him. It weren't no sacrifice. If there was two of me I'd have said, have us both.

—Gloria, he goes. —My beautiful sweetheart. My honey, my babe.

And he takes me in his arms.

But straightaway I know he's different. Not a different man, and not two men exactly – but the same man with different things inside him, some of them mucky and strange.

For once he didn't tell me any stories about what he'd been doing, and how many hits he'd scored.

—This fuckin' war's just gotta end soon, he says, and

there's this clapped-out sound to his voice, hoarse and hot. —All I want's to stay alive and get the hell out soon as I can, back to Chicago, back to pumping gas and fixing automobiles. Jeez, I've lost so many buddies to them fuckin' Germans. You stop giving a shit about guys after a while. Don't get too close to 'em, cos you might lose 'em. I've had it up to here, man.

He's got his crazed look, like someone's told him bad news. The war, I say to myself, the war's told him the bad news – no, the war's rammed it right in his face, that strangers kill each other in cold blood. Who'd be a man?

The war isn't a game for him no more, it isn't no fun, he's seen too many deaths which is what's making him nervy and angry enough to scare me. There's hardly time to get to the bedroom – he half drags me – and it's over in no time, before we've even got our clothes off, still standing up and all, up against the dresser so you can see his backside humping away in the mirror.

Well.

It's OK, I s'pose, cos we both know that later when we do it again we'll be taking our time. And he'll say loving things, not angry crude things, like fuck and bitch, I know it.

After, he opens another bottle of bourbon and we do some drinking, half-naked on the bed, and share ciggie after ciggie, lighting the next one from the last, because he seems to need to smoke a whole pack, lost in a cloud of smoke.

—Say, cutie, he says after he's put out the last stub in the coffee cup. —Let's go to the Mayflower. Get us some chow. Do some jivin'.

And I don't want to say no, because he is the one risks his life every day, not me, so off we go to Marble Arch and eat fish and chips and swarm around with everyone, packed it is, all drunk and flirting and smooching.

The jitterbugging's finished and we're dancing our slow one.

> You had to go, the time was so short,
> We both had so much to say.
> Your kit to be packed, your train to be caught,
> Sorry I cried but I just felt that way.

It's so romantic the whole dance-hall's fainting with it, people hugging and swaying and snogging all around us.
—Did you miss me?
—Dumb question, honey. Sure I missed ya.
His voice is slopping around a bit, and part of the squeezing my waist is to stay upright.

> And now that you're gone, dear, this letter I pen,
> My heart travels with you till we meet again.
> Keep smiling, my darling, and sometime we'll spend
> A lifetime as sweet as that lovely weekend.

—Thanks for looking after Marje, I go. —I don't know how she'd have coped without you.
—She's your sister, hon, he says, as the music fades.
—Anything for a sister of yours.
—Funny, she looks even more like me with her hair that way.
It's true, she's done her hair to look just like mine. It's flattering but it bothers me too, being copied like that.
—Sure you're not a bit gone on her, too?
—Hey. You're my gal, hon! You're my cutie!
The way we were holding each other – Vera Lynn was just starting up – I couldn't see his face but I felt it go hot and we both knew he hadn't answered my question.
—Let's go, I said, dragging him away from the bloody

bluebirds and the bloody white cliffs of Dover, cos I wanted him nowhere else just then but in my bed.

Marje was on night duty. Back at her place again I made him stand there while I looked at him. I couldn't believe how sexy he was, even though he was drunk and couldn't stand straight. We were going to take our time.

—Watch, I said, and I took off my clothes for him, and stood there in front of him with nothing on, and the gas fire glowing blue against the wall, and my love glowing for him. I longed for him, I wanted him to take me.

Slowly, then faster.

—What's the matter? I go.

—Nothing's the matter, hon, he says, rolling his look all over my body, and liking what he saw, which was good tits and curves in all the right places, I had nothing to be ashamed of, I was a looker. And you could see his scar in the firelight, and his thing growing hard again, and so I went up to him because I just had to touch it, it seemed like such a marvel.

—Nothing's the matter, he goes again, everything's fine, hon, you're so sexy, you know that? You're a swell kid, Gloria.

He was hard as a piece of thick rope, and so drunk he was reeling about, but I didn't care, and I didn't care that he didn't have a French letter neither. We were on the floor by now, and his bare chest was making me melt, the sight of it like geography. The muscles on his arms. I ran my tongue across him, I wanted that thing of his inside me.

His eyes were shut.

—I'm going to marry you, honey, he said.

Ah.

I had to shut my eyes so that what he said would echo straight down to my heart. I loved him, I loved him. I ran my tongue further down till I had him in my mouth. He groaned and said lots of things I couldn't hear properly, dirty ugly things, crying out. In my head I blocked my ears to that, and thought about love. *I'm going to marry you, honey.*

Then I sat on him, wet, and slid up his legs and put him in me. We rocked. Slowly, then faster, till I was ready to die with how good it was, and when he started to speak I nearly slapped a hand over his mouth, cos I didn't want to hear no more ugly words. But it wasn't ugly.

—You're coming to Chicago with me, hon.

When he said Chicago he went right in, deeper than he had ever been before, and the word went in with it.

—Are you coming to Chicago?

—Yes. I am, I am.

America was all one place to me, I never thought to look at a map, Chicago sounded like the flicks. Like it was made of gold.

—You try and stop me, I said, and then I locked my mouth on his mouth and my Zedorro Moment was a big swoop, and all the shuddering and shouting I did made him cry out too, a big yelp of man's rage.

And then he cried. He cried and cried, these loud rude sobs, and there was no comforting him, and when I tried to, he pushed me away. Hard.

When I woke up in the early morning Ron wasn't there and the first thing I saw opening my eyes was the bruise on my arm where he'd shoved me. I could hear voices down the hall, so I wrapped myself in a sheet and went over barefoot on the cold floor and there he was in his underwear, arguing with Marje in a big whisper but not loud enough for me to hear the words. She must've just come in from her shift, cos she looked done in and her hair was all frazzled. It shocked me he was just in his underwear like that but maybe he got up to use the lav and she came in. When I made a noise they both turned very fast and said, Hi Gloria, at the same time.

—You two having a row? I asked.

—No, snaps Marje. —It's nothing.

—Just shooting the breeze, says Ron. —Sleep well, Marje.

And he turns to join me, and we go back to bed for one last bit of fooling around before it's time to say goodbye.

He's off on another mission, a long one this time, and he can't tell me what or where, or whether it's from Manston or some other place, and won't look me in the eye, so I know he's scared, scared of dying, and who can blame him, and I'm scared too. I cried my eyes out at leaving him, and at leaving Marje, too, cos she looked worse that morning than she did after she heard the news about Dad and then Bobby.

—You'll always be my sister, she said. —No matter what happens.

—And you'll always be mine, I go, wondering what she means. Has she had a premonition or something?

—Don't get killed on me, Marje. You drive those ambulances safely now. You watch out for them time-bombs, OK?

—Don't worry, she says, I plan to stay alive. Start a new life one day.

—You'll find someone, I go. —Look at you, you're gorgeous. I can just see you starting a new life.

The sight of her mouth, which is Mum's mouth, makes me want to cry more.

—Ron always says we could be twins, she goes.

Funny, but that does a strange thing to me, making me go hot and then cold, so cold I am freezing and numb, and the feeling won't go away, even when I'm waving to her from the train, even when it's pulling back into Temple Meads, even when I get home and into my own bed and listening to Mrs O'Malley yelling at her brats through the wall.

I haven't told her Ron's asked me to marry him. It's too soon after Bobby, and too private – like one of the dirty things he whispers in my ear when we're having it away. But when I think about it – the way he said *Chicago* while he was –

My heart shakes, my insides swoop, I get this lurching low-down feeling that is happiness or panic.

Them black holes in space is the most peaceful places on earth. All that nothing crammed into a hole. I would like to eat one of them holes, or have one of them holes eat me. No room for nothing but nothing then, squash out all the other stuff that comes in, squash it back under the mud down the bottom of the lake.

Yes, I will eat one of them holes one day, I will. Or maybe I will ask one of them holes to eat me.

Don't mind which.

I brought you a lavenderball, says Hank's Wife, handing me this little oily wooden marble. —You put it under your pillow to help you sleep, or in with your underwear.

—What's wrong with a nice bit of muslin with seeds in it?

—Hank's off on the rigs again, she says, fishing about in her handbag.

—Is this one of them three-in-a-bed love triangles then? I go, because here comes the Jill woman who might be a Witness.

—Gloria! she says, still fishing about.

—Well, that's what it looks like from here.

There's a new one, too: a teenage girl with a nose-stud and a slutty tattoo on her arm, holding Calum's hand. Anyone'd think this was one big happy family.

—Talking of which, could you get me and Ed some baby oil?

The lady called Jill has come and sat the other side of me and so has the slutty girl, and they're all looking at each other puzzled.

—Hello, Gloria, goes the Jill woman, deciding not to kiss me but taking my hand and squeezing. —I've brought my daughter Melanie to meet you.

—Hello, goes Melanie, looking at me like I'm something the cat sicked up.

—Watch out for my bones, I tell the Jill woman, who won't let go. —Don't crush them, woman!

She looks like I've slapped her, and the teenager smirks.

—I'll get you some baby oil, she says, but I'll have to write it down or I'll forget. I've a memory like a sieve.

—Join the club, I say.

I mean it to be friendly, but the look she gives me then, it ain't such a nice one, I can tell you.

The handbag-fishing is over, cos Hank's Wife has found what she was after, which is some wooden bits of train-track for the boy. I'm watching telly which is about a South American general, he's a mass murderer, and there's a lot of argy-bargy over how out to lunch he is. There's a man saying he's not as bad as some people would have you believe. Then there's someone got tortured says would you like to look at my scars, he's all tizzed-up and emotional, look, if you will permit I will show them to you now and he starts pulling open his shirt and the interviewer's trying to stop him but before you know it there's his chest scrazzed with wounds like he's been whipped.

—What do you say to that, he says. —Not as bad as some people would have you believe?

—Bloody hell, change the channel will you, goes Ed. —I haven't had my pills yet.

—He should be hanged, says Noreen.

—By the neck, says Ed.

—He's forgotten what he did, goes the Jehovah's Witness woman. —If he's forgotten –

She's talking daft, you can tell she's a loony with those staring eyes.

—Mum, goes Melanie. —What are you talking about? You think he should get away with it? Do you know how many people disappeared under Pinochet?

—Where's Rubber-Lips, anyway? I say, to change the subject.

But when we finally find the remote control under Ed's cushion and then get the right channel, it turns out Marty Lone's in hospital. He's taken a blinking ruddy overdose.

—We're all praying that he'll pull through, says his agent. —He's been under a lot of stress. Marty's someone who's always worked hard and played hard.

That's when I remember the punchline to that joke of Hank's. And don't ask me why, but I feel the need to yell it. Cheer everyone up.

—At least I haven't got cancer!

BOILING SOAP

—Is she still sleeping?

—Or dead. Yoo-hoo, are you dead, Gran?

—Melanie!

—Well? Come on, Mum, would it honestly bother you?

—Yes! It certainly would! She's not getting out of it that easily.

—But what I don't get is, how d'you know she's lying?

—I never said she was lying. What she's doing is not telling the truth. It's not always the same thing. It's a cover-up. Like Watergate, not that you'd know about Watergate.

—Daughtergate!

—You could call it that.

—But why? Why should she go to such lengths? Loads of people gave away their babies after the war. It's not exactly news.

—I don't know. But when you've spent your life –

—Believing in The Missing Link –

—You can laugh, but if it was you –

—Shh! She's waking up.

No I'm not. I'm boiling up my soap in this big iron pot, it's about the only one left, the rest has gone to make aeroplanes and we're permitted one per household so I'm leaning over it reading a letter from Marje, trying not to inhale the stink. This letter, it don't say nothing much, like all her letters since she went to London. It's written in the ambulance while she's parked by a heap of rubble somewhere. Her nurse friend Helen just got married, she says. To a bloke Marje helped pull out of a bombed-out block of flats in Whitechapel. He'd spent three years fighting the Jerries and got injured, lost half a foot. The explosion made him deaf in one ear too but it didn't put Helen off, even with all the offers she got from GIs, cos when they met in the hospital where she was working, and Marje brought him in all covered in blood and brickdust, it was love at first sight. *And you can't fight love*, Marje says. *You have to grab it where and when you can, and if Helen and John are happy together after all they've been through, and can make a life together, good luck to them.* This love-grabbing idea is becoming quite a belief of hers, I'm thinking. This stuff about taking it with both hands and holding on to it for all you're worth, it's –

But I lose track: suddenly, out of the blue, the fumes must be getting to me because there's this vomity feeling welling up, and I go hot and cold.

Something bad has happened, says this little voice inside me. *Don't breathe in the smell. His plane's been shot down. Hold your breath, Gloria. No, he's still here, he's alive, cos I can feel him as close as if he's standing right behind me in the room, stirring the soap with me, breathing in the terrible smell, the worst odour in the world, that makes you want to –*

Oh shit and triple shit, there's no stopping it.

I'm retching so bad I don't have time to put Marje's letter aside, I'm chucking up all over it, and all down my pinny and on to the floor and into the soap-pan, cos that smell don't half make you puke.

Then Mrs Bloody O'Malley only has to come along, just

as I'm dribbling out the last bit where I've staggered out to the back yard.

—Don't think I don't know what you're suffering from, you dirty girl, she calls at me. —You little whore, you've the morals of a slut.

I don't know what she's on about though, do I, I'm that bloody clueless.

The hens are pecking at my sick. Cos hens, they'll eat anything.

The little girl from Gadderton, she's here every night now. She sits on the end of the bed and strings her beads. Don't say nothing. There's a thing I've noticed. She's stringing them on to each other like billy-o, but the string never gets any longer. I could strain my head trying to work this out or I could just say bollocks, and leave it. So that is what I am doing. Saying bollocks to the mystery of her blinking beads. Outside it's blowing a gale round the corners of the block like the windy city of Chicago. I've got the TV on in my room, sound down low, it's some sex thing, that's what they show in the middle of the night, bottoms heaving away like the clappers, you forget the energy you had. But we're not watching, me and the little girl.

We are ignoring each other instead.

Not so easy for me because tonight the little cow is different. Sometimes she is dressed like someone's told her she is a ruddy princess but today she is a mess again, just like the first time at Gadderton, smeared in mud, and dripping water and pond-weed. Next to her there's a raggedy mush of parachute that was once clean and white. It gave me a shock at first but I'm not letting on. It's just to get my attention and I'm not giving her that pleasure, not even complaining about the mess.

—Remember that fish I caught? I say at last above the slap and tickle on the telly. —Remember that fish I caught when we first met, the Hallelujah? I bashed its head till it was pulp.

She turns her head a bit then, looks at me with those teenager eyes. Nods, like she knows already. Bored. Couldn't give a monkey's, could she? Lady Muck, with her chequebook. Something missing, my arse.

In the morning the bed's dented again where she sat and there's a trace of pond-weed and a smear of mud and a smudge of blood like she's had the curse and leaked.

IS NOT A CRIME

You know what Ron used to say? He used to say, *When the shit hits the fan, that's when you gotta keep a tight asshole.*

—I had this copied, Hank says, thought you might like it, to give your memory a jog, and he gives me this photo again, the same one he showed me before.

—Why should I want to give my memory a jog at my age? I go. —Bloody hell, forgetfulness isn't a crime as far as I'm aware.

—Can be, he says. —If it's done on purpose.

And he gives me a not very nice look and buggers off, leaving it on the little table next to the bed, gets back to his tangled love life. The picture shows this woman looks familiar, with a little brat.

Unless bowels move regularly, your child will be weakly, peevish, dull and stunted.

—You take it, I tell the nurse who's Welsh and a foreigner so it's like a double curse. That'll be you in a few months. All alone with a screaming kid, you'll need to give it syrup of figs every day to get its bowels moving, you'll be a slave to them bloody bowels.

—*Xena Warrior Princess* in minute, Gloria, she says. —You favourite programme, I think, no? You want I switch channels?

And now that you're gone, dear, this letter I pen,
My heart travels with you till we meet again.
Keep smiling, my darling, and sometime we'll spend
A lifetime as sweet as that lovely weekend.

This letter I pen, my arse.

There were girls at the factory, they got beautiful letters from their husband or their boyfriend or a man they met at a dance or in the pub. Long letters, and some of them had a pressed flower in that he'd picked on an airfield or somewhere. Me, I wasn't one of them girls. There'd be weeks go by, and I thought: all this time he's got, I know he has spare time, he could be writing to me, not drinking with his mates yakking about planes. But all I get is these little scraps, written in capital letters, like he hasn't learned how to do joined-up writing, and there's always this little twinge of disappointment there when I see how thin the envelope is. One sheet only, and never more than one side of the page. No pressed flowers, just something once that looked like a shred of tobacco but might have been old snot.

Me? I could write him a whole book every night, I could. But because he don't, I don't, or at least I keep them short, shorter than they could be.

Hi there, Honey!

Well, I only have a little time before I take off again, I can't tell you where. My buddy Rowan died in hospital last week, he was wounded real bad. I wrote a letter to his folks which is about the hardest letter I ever wrote. He was some guy. Anyway that's real sad stuff and I don't want to get you feeling blue, when you're already having such a hard time with Mrs O'Malley. Boy, does she sound like a witch. I sure miss you, but I see a lot of Marje when I get into London so it's like having a reminder, and she misses you too, she is still real shook up about Bobby, I guess you know that from her letters. Poor kid, I feel real bad for her. And I feel real bad for me, too, being away from you for so long. But hey, guess what, I have real hot dreams about you, sweetheart, I can't wait to –

And there's four lines crossed out by the censor. *And then you can* – two lines crossed out. They're not supposed to do that, the ruddy spoil-sports. They're not even s'posed to censor letters sent in England, just the ones go abroad. They must be bored out of their stupid tiny minds.

And then lots of kisses at the end, and his name. That was the last letter I got before D-Day. But you know what I'd have liked even more than reading what the censor crossed out? (Because I could guess what was crossed out all right, rude things about different ways he'd like to do it to me.) I'd have liked one of them pressed flowers. Even if it was just a daisy or a dandelion, I'd have liked one. Instead of just some tobacco or snot.

Dear Ron,

I am missing you very much, my darling. And now I have a bit of a surprise for you. We are having a baby. Isn't that great news? The first thing I knew of it was when I was boiling up some cakes of soap and all of a sudden I needed to puke. Now I only feel sick some of the time but that is nothing compared to what you are going through, of course. You are so brave and I am very proud of you, we all are. You will defeat Hitler, I know it! I lie awake at night and think what kind of wedding dress I will have when we get married. Should we do it in Bristol or Chicago? Or maybe London? My tits are swelling by the way, you would like them even more now they are a size bigger and although they hurt a bit

Dear darling Ron,

Every day we are apart is

My dearest beloved Ron,

Remember that night down in London, when we spent the night at Marje's? Well, something happened that night. In fact I am pretty sure it happened just when you asked me to marry you, and come to Chicago with you. We are going to have a

Dear Marje,

There is so much to tell you. First, some very bad news. Remember poor Iris? Well, she took her own life yesterday, by electrocuting herself in the bath using the hand and arm that was left. I have just heard this from her cousin Rose. I am still shaking from it. But I must try to keep calm, and so must you. In fact I hope you are sitting down, because I have some other news, too. You'll never guess what. I've got a bun in the oven! Ron is over the moon, or at least he will be when he gets my letter which I am posting at the same time as yours. We are going to get married and live in Chicago and

Next time Hank comes, he's on about it again. He won't let up, will he.

—Why can't I remember anything about Chicago? he goes.

—Was I a good mum to you Hank? Yes or no?

—Come on, Mum, you know you were.

—Didn't I work hard to give you a nice life? I made us a good home, I did. Took on all them cleaning jobs, even worked Sundays sometimes, you remember. Sang you nursery rhymes, taught you to rock and roll to the gramophone. Took you to Blackpool and Margate and whatnot for your holidays. You could have friends round to play whenever you wanted, you had pocket money for sweets and comics. You did all them Airfix models I paid for, and Meccano. You went to Scout camp, we bought all them Elvis records and sang along.

—Mum. You were a great mum. That's not in dispute. And I'm grateful, I know how much you did for me. I'm just asking you, why can't I remember anything about Chicago?

—Cos you were too young, I tell him. —Babies' minds is just a blur.

—But I was born in London, according to my birth certificate.

—Well, we must've gone to Chicago after.

—How old was I then? And how old was I when we left? And what was so bad about it? Why didn't you and Ron stay together?

Oh bloody hell.

—Can't blinking well remember that far back, can I. Like I always said, things went wrong, it wasn't meant to be.

—I couldn't find your marriage certificate, Mum. Or your divorce papers.

For crying out loud! Isn't a wedding photo good enough for you? If you've been meddling in that bloody box –

—Or your passport.

—Am I supposed to keep everything? Do you keep everything? Was I or was I not a good mum?

—Doesn't matter, says Doris.

—What doesn't?

—That old stuff about papers. What matters is what you did, and you got to tell him, Gloria.

—None of this don't matter, I tell him. —That's what Doris says. Doris says you should let sleeping dogs lie.

—Did not! says Doris. —Said you should stick to what's important. You twist what I say again and I'm gone for good.

—Matters to me, he goes. —It's my life we're talking about.

—No. It was mine. Before you came along.

—And what about Jill Farraday?

—Who's Jill, I don't know no Jill Farraday.

—He means the Jehovah's Witness woman, goes Doris. —With the expensive scarf. The one you don't want to know.

—Your daughter, says Hank. —My sister, or half-sister, or whatever she is. You've admitted she's your daughter, right? So I think the cat's more or less out of the bag, don't you?

—Oh for crying out loud. Look, sonny Jim. D'you think I honestly don't know how many babies I had? D'you think I had a daughter and then just . . . forgot about her? D'you think you weren't enough for me? D'you think it was easy, bringing you up all on my own? Do you know what I had to do, when you was little, before I got the cleaning job at Larman's?

His face goes red.

—OK, Mum, OK. I know it was hard.

—I'll tell you what I did. I had to –

—Mum! He's stood up to go. —Please! I think we can put that behind us!

—You know what I've a good mind to do, I tell him. I've a good mind to go to Ed Mayberley's room right now and see if he's in the mood for it. That so-called sister of yours, she was supposed to get me some baby oil.

That does the trick, he's off like greased lightning, outside for a fag.

—It's all right, I call after him. —I won't charge him for it!

That fat barrage-balloon Mrs O'Malley's got hold of an angora rabbit, she combs it every day listening to the

Horlicks Tea-Time Hour in my kitchen, or sometimes Lord Haw-Haw. She swaps the fur for veg, wormy old carrots or a half a cabbage from a shady-looking bird on Mitchell Street, who makes the fur into collars and whatnot. She keeps this wretched creature in a little hutch out the back yard with my chickens, and puts it on the kitchen table every day to comb.

She's combing the rabbit, wearing her pinny and her fat arms bulging like sausages.

I could steal that bunny, I'm thinking, as I watch her. I light a Craven A and blow the smoke towards her. Sell it on the black market, or swap it for some coupons. Or strangle it.

—Having had six children myself, she goes, combing the creature, I can spot a seven-month pregnancy when I see one.

—It's five, I go, blowing a smoke ring, which is what Ron taught me in bed. —Not seven.

I've hidden it till now – but I'm getting wide and big, though next to her I am thin as a rake of course. I'm eating like there's no tomorrow. Anything and everything I can get my hands on. I even stuffed some earth in my mouth once, I had an urge for it. Ashes too. Remember that tin of peaches in syrup Ron gave me? Well, it's long gone of course but it still pops up in my dreams.

—Five eh, she goes, looking me up and down. —You're in for trouble there.

She combs a bit more, and I don't say anything, just stand there smoking and watching her. I could murder her. I could stub out this ciggie in her eye. Get the poker and stick it in her fat flesh, just between her tits where her heart is meant to be.

—Just declare it and get the extra rations, says Mrs O'Malley. —You'll be doing us all a favour.

But I'm still pretending it's not happening, aren't I. She won't let up though, she's like a dog at a bone.

—I know your game, child, she says, tugging at the comb that's got stuck on a burr. —Blessed Lady Mother of God. (Catholic gobshite comes out of her mouth like drool.)

—What game?

—Prostitution, she says, spitting out the word, full of hate. —They should tar and feather you, you little strumpet. Not even engaged, are you?

That's done it. The bunny's bolted, seeing what's coming before she does. I've thrown myself at her, aiming a punch right in the middle of her fat ugly face, and when it hits there's a slapping noise and then a crunch and my hand's covered in blood and it feels good, so good I'm in the middle of aiming another one, when two of her brats rush in screaming, and tear me off her and pin me to the floor, one on each side. She's screaming and bleeding, and I'm still yelling, still wanting to foul her up more, the bloody parasite bog-trotter, but they've pinned me down, the two lads who is skinny but strong.

—You leave off our ma!

—Or we'll fuckin' kill you, goes the other.

She's wiping at her face with her hands, blood still gushing from her nose.

—As soon as Ron comes back, I yell at her, I'll tell him everything you said! Then you'll pay for calling me a whore, you evil old bog-trotter!

—We'll see about that, she chokes, cos the barrage balloon's got to have the last word, hasn't she, even with the blood streaming. —We'll see about him coming back.

I make to lunge at her again, but the brats won't let me up off the floor and my heart isn't in it any more to be honest, I'm that done in and beat, and so I flop and just stay there, rabbit-fur flying all around, and the chicken-droppings, and when they've gone off to clean up their fat bog-trotter barrage balloon ma, I just sit there on the floor with my legs sprawled wide and my tummy bulging over, and I bawl like a blinking baby.

—What d'you call a reindeer with no eyes?

Doris groans, cos I have told her this one before.

—No-eye Deer, she says. —Now listen, Glor. I have been meaning to have a talk with you.

—Oh lawks, spare us, would you!

—I am trying to help you, I really am. Listen, when you're dead you see how small you were and how it was all a bit of nonsense really. I mean it, Glor. You got too much pride, you have. You live in the world, and there's thousands and millions of other people all living their lives, some of them good lives and some of them bad lives, and they all end up same as me at the end of the day. But there's ways you can make it easier on yourself before you go, everyone can. And now's the time for you to do that. It's more difficult for you, Glor, cos not all of the mess was your fault. But you need to say sorry to Jill, you do. That's what I'm saying. You don't even know what for, and maybe you never will, but take it from me, you'll both feel better for it. Apologise to her for what you did.

This dead woman is off her blinking trolley.

—How can I say sorry if I ain't done nothing?

—But you did something, Gloria. You may not remember what, but you still got a conscience, you still know deep inside that you did something evil.

—My arse! I know nothing of the sort!

She sighs.

—Oh well. Hey! She points at the TV; it's Rubber-Lips. —Look! Marty's out of rehab.

And so it gets dropped, not a minute too soon for me, because it ain't half stirred up a bad feeling in me.

Marty's mum's back to nursing him at home, just the

two of them, it says. And then there's a clip of Marty. He's had to sort out a lot of issues, he says, and take some difficult stuff on board, but he's a better person in himself for what he's been through, though he wouldn't recommend it.

—I should coco!

There's a little silence, and Doris goes all watery-looking, like she'll disappear. But she doesn't; she's just fainter.

—What's it like being dead then? I ask Doris.

—Not much different, she says, though I notice she's wearing a nice smart jacket, must've cost her.

—I'm in no hurry, I tell her.

—Just as well, says Doris, cos you've not finished what you started. And you can't go till you have.

—Will it hurt?

But she don't say nothing.

—Will it kill me? The room's gone quiet, so quiet you can't even hear your own heartbeat, and you can't see her no more neither.

And I am all of a sudden hungry for a black hole.

Mrs O'Malley was wrong to accuse me of being on the game, cos that didn't happen till later. So she was in a time muddle, wasn't she?

After the bust-up with her, I got a fright, because who did I bump into in the street downtown but the Great Zedorro. I'd just bought some lilac from a gypsy boy, fourpence a bunch and I can't resist lilac, specially when it's that strong mauve and smells so sweet. I couldn't afford it, with the factory closed for a week because of faulty pipes, and no pay, but sometimes a girl needs a treat.

I was going to say hello this time, instead of following him like a German spy. Because it's a lonely business having your mum and dad dead and a sister gone away and girls in the factory saying, if he's your fiancé, how come you ain't got a ring? Jewellery not permitted, I say, remembering Iris's hand and arm. Our troops are rounding up Jerry, we've bombed Dresden and had the glory of D-Day and Hitler's getting his comeuppance, and a letter from Ron is probably already in the post and we're all just waiting for this blinking war to be over with.

—Mr Zedorro? I went, tapping him on the shoulder. It was like the lilac, I couldn't resist.

He almost jumped out of his skin.

—Oh, he goes, not looking too pleased to be recognised. —I've . . . left Zedorro behind for now. He checks to see who's around, but no one is. —Call me Bill.

—Bill, I said. It didn't sound right, after Zedorro. As in, a bit of a come-down, for the man who persuaded me I was a human rod of iron and put oranges on my tummy and had a whole theatre on their feet and cheering and believing his hocus-pocus was for the glory of Britain. —So what are you now? I go. —I mean, what do you do?

—Oh, I left ENSA, he says, walking on. I walk on with him, he's not getting away from me that easy now I've recognised him. —Got called up to work for the Ministry of Defence, he says. Nice flowers you've got there.

—Lilac. Doing what?

He sucks in his breath.

—Careless talk costs lives, he goes, lips all thin. —I'm sorry. I can't tell you.

—You hypnotise people? Is that what you do still?

He's walking faster now but I'm not letting him go, so I speed up too even though I am huffing and puffing with the baby-weight because I am blinking enormous, I am.

—Do you remember me?

—Of course, he goes, I never forget a face. (He's smiling now, proud of this.) —Miss Gloria Double-U. Winstanley, isn't it? How long has it been?

—More than a year, I tell him. Eighteen months, maybe?

—A lot of water under the bridge since then, he says.
—For both of us. And now you're in trouble.

—No, I go. It's not trouble, it's happy. I've got a fiancé. Ron.

—The gentleman you came to see the show with? The handsome GI? Well, congratulations, he goes. —When's the wedding?

—It's not fixed yet, I tell him. In fact I –

There's this thing in my throat that stops more words escaping. I go hot, and I nearly walk off there and then, I know what he must be thinking. But something keeps me there, because he's looking at me, his head on one side, like a bird. For some reason I want to cover up my tits, which are suddenly feeling too pregnant-looking, so I shift my bunch of lilac, the stalks wrapped in soggy newspaper with pictures of Hitler on. He's older than when he was up there on the stage with the Slut Fairy, and his hair's got grey in it. He's just ordinary now. He's just a man, like any man. You could think less of him.

—You haven't told him yet, have you, he says.

How does he know? How does he know I never posted none of them letters?

—When the war's over, I start to tell him.

Zedorro nods.

—Course. Wait till after the war. Nice surprise for him. You won't be alone. (It's true. There's plenty being born out of wedlock.) He gives a little chuckle. —I saw a young miss only the other week pushing a pram, with a black one in it. Never seen that before, a white girl and a black baby. Took me a while to work it out!

That eases things up, and we get walking in rhythm, me lighting up a Craven A. I offer him one but he don't smoke.

—Next time Ron's back on leave is when I'm doing it, if the war isn't over first, and they say it won't be long.

Then we can start our lives again in Chicago. But I'm not telling Marje – she's my sister – till I've told Ron.

Seen Ron's face, is what I'm thinking. Get him to wear a French letter, she said. You don't want a bun in the oven.

—There's no need to explain, he goes. —With a war on . . .

We walk on a bit, saying nothing, and when we reach Leavesden Avenue, he says —This is where I turn off. Where are you headed?

—Nowhere much, I tell him. —The factory's closed this week and my house is full of Catholics.

—Come back for tea then, he says. —Meet my wife. Would you care to?

—What for? I go, not realising quite how rude it sounds. But he don't take offence.

—Just a suggestion. But – well. I get the feeling you don't have many people to talk to. With your sister in London and your fiancé away?

He is a kind man but he is clever too. Watch out. But the kindness wins me over after Mrs O'Malley, and I say thanks, I'd love to, and we walk down Leavesden Avenue, and I pretend I've never seen his house before cos I'm not letting on I spied on him, and I say what a nice road, I have never been here before, and we go in.

The Slut Fairy don't look like the Slut Fairy no more, she's regular-featured but nothing special, and the jealousy I had, it's gone. *It's That Man Again*'s playing on the wireless but she's not laughing, she looks sad – and when she sees my big belly she makes a face and flashes Zedorro a look, then switches the wireless off.

—Hello, Mrs Zedorro, I go. Then something comes over me and I shove the lilac at her and say —For you.

—Oh they're lovely, are you sure? she goes. —You can call me Grace.

—Gloria Winstanley, I tell her.

—Yes, she smiles, smelling the lilac, and I can see she can't resist them neither. —I remember. You came to one of our shows.

—You were very suggestible, says Zedorro.

—I still am, I go.

Not quite knowing what I mean by it.

—People either are or they're not, he goes. —Some of the people I work with, there's no point even trying. Others, you have a result straightaway. This project I'm –

—Bill, goes Grace, with a warning in her voice. —You're not supposed to – (She looks at me.) —He's not supposed to talk about his new work, she goes. —It's top secret.

—Say no more, I go, and we share a woman's glance and then she gets up and says she'll just nip out to the kitchen and pop these in a vase, and make a pot of tea.

—Tell us more about your fiancé, says Zedorro who is called Bill, when we are gathered round the pot giving it time to brew before she pours. She's put the vase of lilac on a wooden chest and they look so good I'm regretting being generous.

—Ron's in the air corps, I tell them. —He's been on flying missions over Germany but I've heard nothing since before D-Day. I'm sick with worry, expecting news he's been shot down, but nothing's getting through. He might even be in America, for all I know, if he's been injured. They send them back, you know.

—It's hard, isn't it, says the Slut Fairy who is called Grace. —I know Bill's dying to talk about what he's been doing with his patients, but you can't be too careful.

—Patients? I go.

Because there's a convalescent home set up just outside Bath.

—There I go, she says, slapping a hand over her mouth. —Careless talk! So when is your baby due?

The siren went off then, so we had to raise our voices to talk over it, but Grace, she'd gone all pale.

—I hate that noise, she goes. —That swoop, and then the howl. It turns my stomach.

—It's OK, dear, says Bill. —Don't panic now. She worries. Her friend was killed.

—I used to ignore them like everyone else, she says, but I can't any more, even though there's so few of them now. In fact the fewer there are, the worse it is.

—If you can hear them landing, you're safe, I say. —It's when you can't hear them that you cop it.

—Let's go to the shelter, says Grace. —Please?

So seeing as I am their guest, and it seems rude not to, off we go outside to the public shelter in Harper Square and they take their two gas-masks with them and we file in, along with everyone else, some with thermoses and sandwiches, and plenty in curlers and house-coats. It stinks of old piss down there of course, and I always hated the places but there we are stuck together till the all-clear sounds, with our gas-masks, looking like a herd of bloody elephants.

—My friend who was killed, goes Grace, wrinkling up her nose at the piss stink. (We're huddled in the corner, the three of us, a little apart from the rest of them on benches, some of them eating or trying to kip down.) —She had her baby with her. The baby was killed too. We'd been to see *Gunga Din* at the Regent, and we heard the sirens, but didn't think much of it. But afterwards, when we saw the ambulances were heading towards Meadow Road –

—Shh, goes Bill. —No need to dwell.

—I never used to be nervous, murmurs Grace. —I wasn't the type.

She has good bone structure, she does.

—War changes everyone, says Bill.

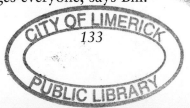

133

We have dropped our voices low, so the conversation's just a murmur in the candles.

—I've changed, I say, but I don't know if it's the war.

—I've seen it bring out the best and the worst, says Bill. —My patients, they've seen things they can't live with. Done things too sometimes. Sometimes they can't even talk about it. But more often than not they can't stop. It's a nightmare world for them, they're re-living it over and over again. There's this one man, Navy captain, he had to finish off his own –

—Bill! goes Grace sharply. —Careless talk.

—I'm helping them, he says. —That's all. It's not a national secret.

—You signed the Act, she hisses, looking anxious. —Now tell us about your sister, Grace says, to change the subject. And so I start off on Marje but soon enough I end up crying, don't I, and telling them about my fight with the barrage balloon.

—You come to us if you ever need any sort of help, goes Bill.

—Why should I need help?

—You never know, he says. —You'd be surprised how many people do. Anything you need, he says. —Don't hesitate.

—We could look after your baby for you, blurts Grace. —If you wanted.

—Until you're back on your feet again. Grace does some war work but she could help out, couldn't you, darling?

—Yes, says Grace, her eyes gleaming and those cheek-bones jutting in the light. —Please, don't hesitate. We mean it, Gloria. We'll do whatever we can. We love babies, don't we?

And I could see that was true, and see from the sadness that they couldn't have one of their own. We all must have slept for a while, because the next thing I knew the all-clear was sounding and everyone started packing up their stuff and trooping out into the morning air, and when the three of us said goodbye, I felt a weight had been lifted, because Zedorro and the Slut Fairy were OK, they were even probably people you could trust, if you were the trusting type. And how many of them are there around?

LIKE WE ARE CHILDREN

Christmas is coming so Conchita la Paz is putting up the decorations because she is a practising Catholic and Mrs Manyon says the baubles will cheer her up. She's homesick for Abroad. There's a plastic tree for later, we'll all decorate it together like we are children, but children who are going to die. And Conchita's hung stuff from the ceiling with Sellotape, and Mrs Manyon has bossed her, and her eyes have gone wet and she has gone to look for some scissors but she will go in the little room where they keep the bedpans and snivel instead.

One of the angel fish has croaked, full of the gas of death, I found it floating. Doris has teamed up with the little Gadderton Lake girl, and they're both staring at it. The kid's still got that Lady Muck look. I want to fish it out but Ed says leave it be, Mrs Manyon'll see to it, and Noreen who hardly ever speaks pipes up to agree, but I've got the lid off the tank and if I reach in with a knitting needle I can skewer it like a kebab.

—What are you doing there, goes the Jill woman who is wearing a knitted jersey thing today that is posh colours, mauve and green, like a sea-anemone I once saw in an aquarium with Hank.

—What's it look like I'm doing? I rake around with the needle, size eight, skewer it and show her the dead body.

Angel fish are flat as a pancake normally speaking but this one's got a bulge.

—Full of the gas of death, see?

—It might be pregnant, she says.

—Then I've put it out of its misery then, haven't I.

She looks at me like I'm the devil.

Some tinsel comes unstuck from its Sellotape and drops to the floor, but she don't go and pick it up. This tinsel, it's green and silver. Tinsel gets thicker every year. The tinsel Hank and I used to have for our little tree, it was like straggly old wool, hardly any twinkle to it. This tinsel is quality, this tinsel –

—There's a specialist coming from London to see you, she says, voice all chilly again, she's a right Lady Muck, she is. —He's due on Thursday.

—Specialist? What kind of specialist?

—An expert on memory loss, she goes. —Hysterical amnesia, Alzheimer's, that sort of thing.

—My memory's not lost, I go. —It hides sometimes, that's all. It's normal in the elderly.

—Yes, isn't that handy, she says, and looks at me all funny, which makes me glad she's no relation of mine because I am beginning to think she is worse than the other one, in other words a right bloody stuck-up Lady Muck bitch. And sometimes, with that mouth of hers, she looks so much like Marje that I could slap her.

—Tell us a joke then, I go.

—You like jokes, do you, Gloria?

—As it happens, I do. Got one then? Got one for me?

Course she bloody hasn't. Marje never could remember none either.

Dear Little Sis,

   Sorry I haven't written for such a long time but we

have all been so busy! I haven't had a day off in weeks. London is still such a mess – rubble everywhere and so many casualties. My friend Angela got caught by an incendiary and died four days ago from the burns. It was awful. I just want this war to end. And do you know what I want to do? I want to leave this country. Frankly I don't care if I never see it again.

Anyway, Gloria, I must rush now. I actually have some quite big news, but you know me – I want to tell you in person. It's too important to say in a letter and it's something we need to talk about, you and I. That's all I'll say for now.

Your sister always,
Marjorie.

Big news? Well, that makes two of us. And mine's the size of a whale.

Hitler's dead, shot himself in a bunker with Eva Braun. Wonder if they fucked first.

War's over soon then – but you wouldn't know it at the factory which has opened up again cos they've fixed the pipes, and we're back on ten-hour shifts working like billy-o, but Mr Simpson says I can do six what with my condition, if I'll take a pay cut. Well, I don't have much choice in the matter, do I, cos I'm so big now I can't stand on my pins all day, so six it is.

Not long now I s'pose before the order comes to stop making bombs and make something else such as prams, cos the war'll be over.

I'm in an orange turban this morning, doing six till twelve, and Maisie and I are just on to the second verse of 'We'll Meet Again' when sure enough Mr Simpson sounds the bell and tells us we can all go home, Mr Churchill is expected to make an announcement shortly, and Maisie and I grin all over our faces, cos we know what this is going to be, don't we, the rumours have been buzzing all week and now it's going to happen.

Back home I'm still all afidget with it, can't keep still even though the baby's weighing me down. I'm ready to pop but there's still a month to go by my reckoning – the day it was conceived being the last time I saw Ron.

So there I am in the kitchen fidgeting and fussing, while Mrs O'Malley combs her blasted rabbit, which I keep thinking about how to strangle. Would it be as easy as a chicken? You could make a good stew from a creature like that. Carrots and potatoes, you'd put in. Some chicken stock.

—You won't be needing him much longer, I told her.
She snorts.
—Sure I will, girl. You think the shortages are going to end with the war? You're even dafter than I thought, child.
—You'll have to leave my house, I told her. —As soon as this war's over, you're out. Might mean tomorrow.
—And what'll you do for money, she goes. —Who'll be paying you rent when I'm gone?
—My sister'll be coming back. And we'll get a lodger for our mum and dad's room. A single person, a single lodger. Just one room, we'll give him.
—Him?
—Or her. Anyway that'll be for Marje to deal with cos I'm off to Chicago.

She carries on combing her rabbit, which must like the feeling because he just sits there, letting it happen.
—We'll see, she goes. —We'll see what the situation is like when you have a babby on your hands. We'll see about Chicago.
And she smirks.
—I'm going out, I say all of a sudden, cos I've had enough, and I can't stand to sit there watching her

wretched comb go up and down on the rabbit, and feel myself fidgeting, fidgeting, and itching to strangle the thing and get a good meal down me.

—Good idea, she says. —Get yourself some fresh air. Read your letter from America.

What?

And slowly, she reaches in the pocket of her pinny. Pulls out an envelope. The evil fucking bog-trotting cow! Who does she think she is?

—How long have you had that? I go, lunging forward to grab it.

—Not so fast, she goes, pulling it away and holding it high so I can't reach. —It arrived last week. Or was it the week before, now? Let me think, I can't recall. Maybe last month? Put it in my pocket and forgot all about it!

And she laughs like it's funny to be that cruel.

How dare she! How dare she sit on a letter of mine! A letter from Ron! I'm ready to burst with the rage, I am, but I don't want no more fist-fighting, being so preggers, so I just snatch the letter out of her fat hand and rush out, stumbling off down the street. On and on I am stumbling, the letter clutched in my hand so I'm crumpling it, but I can see through the blur of my tears it's Ron's writing, and it's posted from America, so he's alive, he's alive, and this is him saying, Come to Chicago, honey. Come and marry me, come to Chicago, and I'm laughing through my tears, laughing and laughing with the relief of it. I'm a swell kid, I am.

Where am I? I look about and see that I'm in Percy Street, heading for Leavesden Avenue, to see Zedorro and the Slut Fairy, and I notice that there's people hurrying all over the place, and there's a man shouting something I can't hear, and as I make my way towards Zedorro's house, I'm feeling right odd, and I'm guessing it's because Ron's alive and I've got his letter to prove it, and the war's ending, cos you can feel things like that through your skin. By the time I get to the door I'm shaking, and there's this pain low down, a very bad backache that has struck.

It's Grace who opens the door. Her eyes widen a bit because of the state I'm in, the letter being waved in her face and the tears, but she don't say a word, just leads me in the house and sits me on the sofa, and the wireless is on loud.

—Mr Churchill's going to come on, she says. —The war's ending.

She's jittery, she's got this huge smile, her eyes are shining, her hands are all afidget.

—Ron's written me a letter, look, I go.

—Oh I'm pleased, she says. —I knew he would. And she puts her finger to her lips because she wants to hear Winnie's announcement. Then I get a sharp pain.

—I think it's happening, I tell her. —Bloody hell, it's not meant to! Not for another month!

She looks up, puzzled, like she's forgotten my condition.

I cry out. There's violence swarming through me, like the curse but a thousand times worse, like you're going to split right open. That's when I know it ain't no false alarm, and my scream drowns out the wireless, and this frightened look whips across her face. Then there's a little lull as the pain dies back, and I can breathe normal again and she can wipe my face with a hankie. But before I know it, along comes another one, the worst kind of pain I have ever felt, a huge wave of it, welling up and reaching such a pitch that I'm screaming again, screaming for it to stop.

She leaps up, settles me back on the settee, does things with cushions and a glass of water.

—Stay there, she says. —I'm going for a doctor.

She's halfway out the door when some music comes on

the radio, and it takes me a minute to realise it's 'God Save the King'. She stops.

—It's happening, she says, her face lighting up. —The war! They're going to say it's ending!

So bloody what, I think, the end of the war ain't nothing compared to the pain I'm in. Then I get another wash of it and I'm howling like a banshee, and yes, all of a sudden, the war news is just a bit of background bother to me, even when Winnie who admired my onions comes on, saying, *German armed forces surrendered unconditionally on May 7th. Hostilities in Europe ended officially at midnight, May 8th, 1945. Yesterday morning at 2.41 a.m. at headquarters, General Jodl, the representative of the German High Command* . . . and she's dancing around, excited about the war ending, annoyed about me spoiling it for her. She's panicking too, you can tell. But I need her.

—Help me, I go. —I am in bloody agony here, I am.

—Look, I'm going for a doctor. Can I leave you here while I go for one? I'll have to get to a telephone, or I'll just go to the surgery and –

—You'll come back! Tell me you're coming back!

—Of course, she goes. —Don't worry, Gloria. Hold tight there now, I'll do what I can.

—Bloody hell, just go, woman!

And she's off like greased lightning. I tear the letter open between the swoops of pain and try to read it but I can't make sense of it. None of the words is in the right order or even saying the right things. It is all wrong, it don't make no sense, it can't even be from Ron, even though the writing's his.

Today, perhaps, we should think of ourselves, says Winnie. *Tomorrow we shall pay a particular tribute to our Russian comrades, whose prowess in the field* . . .

It's good news, isn't it. It means I can go and join Ron in Chicago and be a GI Bride, and we can live happily ever after. I carry on screaming and howling with the pain of the baby, and the relief about Ron, and the fear about me, cos I'm thinking I will die.

Advance, Britannia! says Winnie. *Long live the cause of freedom! God save the King!*

The girl from Gadderton was crying in the night. Crying her little eyes out, and stringing her beads. I thought of going to comfort her but then I thought better of it. It'd only encourage her.

We're decorating the tree with some of the old folk have got diseases. At least the tree's not a real one, we won't be sweeping up needles day and night. But Conchita la Paz is still off for a dustpan and brush because I dropped a glass ball that smashed, and the bits is everywhere. Ed's helping too, he's very jolly today, he is. He's wound tinsel round his Zimmer for that festive look.

—Are you a Jap? he asks Conchita la Paz, and she laughs and shakes her head. —Cos I hate them bastards.

—Where d'you stay then, a hotel? I ask the Jehovah's Witness woman, who's round here every day now, clearly nothing better to do.

—With Hank and Karen, she goes. —They've very kindly been putting me up. And Melanie, too, when she comes.

—Who's Melanie?

—My daughter.

—The slutty one?

She stops, holding a little gold reindeer that's meant to be hung. There's a bit of wall she looks at sometimes, over by the fish-tank.

—I have your old room, she goes, after a while. Then looks for somewhere to hang the reindeer.

—Bitch!

—Pardon?

—That's my bloody room, that is, it'd still be mine if they hadn't stuck me in here.

She's found a branch for the reindeer and now she's inspecting some plastic holly, disapproving of it because it don't have no class.

—Dr Kaplan's coming this afternoon, she goes.

—I've got nothing to hide, I tell her. —My past is an open book.

She's looking at her bit of wall again. Hasn't even got a pattern on it but she don't care.

I feel Doris's eyes on me but she don't say nothing so I don't say nothing back.

What no one ever tells you is that you'll always be alone, trapped inside yourself for ever. It's like a house you were born in, and some of the furniture belonged to your mum and dad but you can chuck that out if you want to, or if you can. But you've got to bloody well live in this house, that's the thing. Even if it's a hole and you prefer the look of other people's. Nobody tells you how it's going to be, living inside yourself. How grey things'll look from your window, if that's the mood you're in. But when you close the curtains it's worse.

—I brought you that baby oil you asked for, she goes, after a bit of silence. —You sure you wouldn't prefer moisturiser?

—No, baby oil's better for what Ed and I have got in mind, isn't it, Ed? I call across as she hands it to me. That's when she nearly grabs it back but I've got it.

—She's a right goer, your old mum, goes Ed, leaning on his tinselly Zimmer. —Your room or mine, Gloria? Glorious Gloria, I call her.

—But you can't –

—There's certain things you have to grab while you can, missis, and this is one of them, I tell her. —Hey,

Ed, stop fiddling with yourself, you old monkey. Now if you'll excuse us, I go. —You can carry on with this tree, or there's plenty of magazines you can look at, I bet you like those posh country-home ones.

She's starting to look ill. Hasn't got no poise, that one.

DR KAPLAN COMES TO PLAY

—Shepherd's pie for lunch, announces Mrs Manyon. Followed by kiwi flan. Countdown to Christmas, she goes, winking at the foreign girls.

I'm reading *Hello!* magazine but it's out of date. It shows Rubber-Lips smiling after rehab but by the time it was in the shops, he'd taken another overdose. I saw on the news. He's in intensive care.

—He doesn't look so good from where I'm sitting, says Doris. —All those regrets he's got about stuff he didn't say to people. You don't want to be in that position, Glor. You don't want to die with things left unsaid. Take it from me.

—His poor old mum, I say, not liking this theme of hers. —You put all that effort into a boy, struggle to bring him up, feed him syrup of figs, work your backside off, make all those sacrifices –

—Who are you talking to there, Gloria, goes Mrs Manyon.

—Doris.

—Doris? she goes, then pats my arm all soft. —Poor Gloria, you miss her, don't you?

—Not really.

—That's what you say, says Mrs M. —But I know better.

—She always did, goes Doris, and then in comes the dinner-trolley, and uh-oh, the Jill woman's back, in a posh cardie. And I'm just eyeing a plateful of flan, scrumptious with custard, and she's got a man with her from Watchtower Headquarters, and the slutty daughter with the nose-stud.

—How much d'you pay for a cardie like that then? Fifty quid? A hundred?

—This is Dr Kaplan, she goes. —It's cashmere.

—How much?

—Hello, Mrs Taylor, mind if I call you Gloria? goes the man.

—Help yourself, I don't stand on ceremony.

—Hello, Gran, says the slutty girl.

—But you can call me Mrs Taylor. Bloody cheek.

Scruffy-looking, this Dr Kaplan. Looks more like a tramp than a specialist, with his scruffiness.

—Are you a Jew? I go.

—A pleasure to meet you, Gloria, he goes, holding out a hand that's got no bones in it. I make a kind of noise, not quite hello because I can't be buggered, my teeth are giving me gyp and I had a bad night with the little girl accusing me of this and that, it's all in her head, and the second angel fish has died, grieving for the first one maybe or ate some bad flakes.

—Them Jews, they're always on about the war, I tell him. But they weren't the only ones suffered. Every chance they get and they're raking over that Holocaust of theirs, they won't blinking well let go of it. It's unhealthy. They should look to the future a bit more. Get some fresh air into their systems. It's not healthy, living in the past.

—An interesting theory, says Dr Kaplan.

What a polite boy.

There's a bit of silence, and then the Jill Farraday woman says —We'll leave you together for a little chat then, and she goes off in her cashmere, and the teenage girl shoots me a dirty scornful look and follows, shuffling on her shoes which is practically stilts.

—Not like Jill to miss out on anything, I tell the doctor.

He just smiles. He's young but he looks older than he is which is I don't know what age. Like an old man shrunk down, balding head, little rimless glasses to make him think he looks clever. Interesting I should mention the Jews, because he's got a theory about the function of memory, he's saying. A theory that we are our memories.

—That memory is what we are, because we have no identity without memory. Our consciousness is a collection of things we have remembered. You know, history, general knowledge, practical expertise, our own life story and emotional past . . . When you think about it, personality without memory is like –

—Fish without chips, I go, to shut him up. (What's he doing all the talking for, I thought it was my shout.) —Chips without ketchup. Ketchup without . . . fish.

He smiles.

—Oh, it can be worse. It can be like nothing. It can be like a void. Some people suffer from something called fugue. It's a clinical pathological loss of memory.

—If you came here to put the frighteners on me, it ain't working.

—Why would you think I came here to – put the frighteners on you?

—How far d'you come then?

—From London.

—Train or car?

—By train.

—Two hours is it still? I used to do that trip. They got a buffet car or do they come round with a trolley? Sandwiches and a cup of tea?

—Tell me, Gloria, are you happy here?

—Happy? What sort of question's that?

—Chicago, says Dr Kaplan, changing the subject.

—The windy city, I go.

—And what else?

—Dunno. Saw it on a documentary once. Just an American city, isn't it, a typical American city.

—Do you remember what state it's in?

—Not a bad state. Not bad at all. Why are you asking? He sighs.

—I just wonder how much you remember of it. You spent time there, as I understand it.

—Never been there in my life.

—That's not what you told your son.

—What is this, the bloody Spanish Inquisition?

—Do you tend to forget things, Gloria?

—Course I do, I'm old, aren't I. It's my right.

—Your choice too, he goes.

—Are you a Jew?

—What I was trying to say to you, Gloria, is that our memories are part of being human. Memory is part of our humanity. Who is Gloria Taylor without her memories? Who am I without mine, or without the history of my own family?

—Come again?

—Memory can be a blessing, but it can also be a curse. Some people feel so cursed that they persuade themselves to suppress whatever memory is haunting them. (Blah blah blah, he likes the sound of his own voice don't he.) —What's interesting to me is the way people can sometimes remember events they thought they'd forgotten. Something will just pop up, out of the blue.

—Iris. Girl called Iris got blown up in the factory. She popped up. Out of the blue.

—Yes. You see? And you've probably noticed that

your short-term memory gets worse while your long-term memory improves. You reminisce. Now tell me, Gloria, you must have thought about America from time to time. Where did you live, when you were in Chicago?

I know it's a trap, a doctor's trap, but I don't know what kind, just know he's on the lookout and leading me into it and I'd better watch it, I reckon, so instead of Chicago I tell him about a recipe that I got from a magazine.

—It's called Mallow Mash. It's American, it's potato with marshmallow in and you do it in the microwave. Modern American cooking, it said. Not that they cook much except pot roast or Thanksgiving turkey which was what Ron was forever on about in November.

But his Jewish eyes glaze over. Try something else then.

—How d'you know when a girl from Barnsley's had an orgasm? Eh? She drops her chips.

But he don't laugh.

—Gloria, I have to say I think you are avoiding my question.

—I said she drops her chips! It's a joke!

—I asked a question.

—Which is what, I go, cos I've forgotten, I'm a sieve.

The sheer truth. But Doris don't like it one bit. She has wafted her way in and so has the little Gadderton girl to give me a hard time, and she has poked me in the ribs and I make a yelp from the pain.

—Lay off!

—A twinge of something, Gloria? goes Dr K.

—She poked me, I go.

—Who?

—Spit it out, says Doris. —I have warned you and warned you about telling porkies.

—Doris who is dead.

—I see, he goes, clearly does not. A little silence and then he says —Where you lived in Chicago – I mean, Gloria, am

I actually right in thinking that you have at least *been* to Chicago? It's something I'd like to unpack.

Unpack?

—A sieve, mate. Sorry.

I tell him this over and over, *a sieve, a sieve*. And Doris and the little girl join me helpless and angry but we are all sieves, I tell them, can't you see, sieves is how we end up and I am at the ending-up end of life.

He sighs.

—Would you say that your past has left you in peace, Gloria?

—Pretty much.

—And that you have – made your peace with it?

—Are you telling me I'm going to die? Cos if you are, you've come a long way to announce me what isn't news, mate. Dr Kaplan, this is an old people's home. When you leave here, it ain't on rollerskates.

—What I'm trying to find out, Gloria, he goes, is this one thing. The episodes in your life that you've forgotten. Did you forget them because you're becoming, er – forgetful? Or did you forget them . . . before that?

—Can't remember, can I?

Doris and the little girl is still watching from the corner but he's not aware of course, being medical. So on and on it goes, round in circles, poor Dr Kaplan, poor me, till he looks at his watch, time's up.

When Dr Kaplan's spoken with the Jill woman, she gives this big sigh and shoots me a glare, don't say nothing. So I borrow a Zimmer because this session has right knackered me, and I clank off, leaving the two of them together, murmuring their Jehovah's Witness prayers.

Ed's room is number 44. I park the Zimmer outside, open the door quiet in case he's off in the land of Nod. And sure enough there's this little hump shape in the bed, which is him. It's like he's been waiting for me, cos he's there asleep with his little portable TV on, and when I lift back the cover which is a nice bedspread, lilac and purple with little flowers, girly you'd say for a man, I see he's just got his jim-jam top on but no bottoms, the dirty old monkey, and before I've got time to think I'm unscrewing the baby oil that we keep on his bedside table, and taking off bits of my own clobber and shoving him along a bit to snuggle down with and he wakes up and says —Well, if it isn't Gloria, and I say —Well, if it isn't Ed, and nothing much happens though we have another go, but we're sweethearts now, aren't we.

—No one can force me to remember stuff, can they? I go, rubbing his bald old tummy after we've given up trying.

And he says —No, Gloria, your mind's the one thing you've got left that's your own, and you keep it that way. Don't you let them say otherwise and don't you let them take it away from you neither.

And he takes one of my tits in his hand and starts sucking at it like an old babby that needs milk to go to sleep.

The little Gadderton Lake girl is bleeding on to my bed again in the night, bleeding out of her nasty little fanny on to my nice coverlet.

—Get off, I'm telling her. —Get your bleeding fanny off my bedspread.

Dr Nosy Parker comes again the next day or whatever day it is. On and on, it goes. Questions about the war, what I did and all, and when I get to the Great Zedorro he gets excited.

—The great who?

—Zedorro.

—A hypnotist, you say?

I tell him about the show he did that Ron and I went to,

which had such an effect on us. I tell him about the bowl of oranges on my tummy, and about meeting him later in Bristol with the Slut Fairy, and him and her being kind to me, but I can't remember how.

—What happened to him? Did you stay in touch?

—I don't know.

—And Ron? he says, getting out a letter.

My heart thuds. Is he trying to kill me?

It's an old letter because it's yellow, and there's an American stamp, and the postmark is Chicago. He don't do nothing with it, just shows me he's got it. I haven't seen it in years, but I know it by heart, and all of a sudden everything's a jumble and I'm in tears, and my thoughts are running all over the place like a spell's been broken and a jinx let out.

—Are you trying to kill me?

—Of course not. I'm sorry, he goes. —Forgive me. I –

—You're not a doctor, I go, heart still banging. —You're a bloody fraud, let's see your credentials then.

He smiles at that, a sorry-missis kind of a smile, and hands me his card which I can't read without my glasses as he well knows.

—We could try and find out what happened to Zedorro, he says. —Though of course he may well be dead. You say he was quite a bit older than you? If you were in your twenties, was he, say, in his thirties? Forties?

The thought that he might be dead makes me feel relieved, don't ask me why.

—Was Zedorro his real name? Or was it just what he used . . . on stage?

—I never knew his real name. Or if I did I've forgotten. He was just called Bill.

—Bill, he says, writing it down and thinking about it.

—And the Slut Fairy, she was called Grace.

He looks up sharply.

—Are you sure? The couple were called Bill and Grace?

—Course I'm bloody sure. Who murdered Zedorro anyway? I go. (Don't know if I want to hear or not.)

He leans forward, eyes all eager behind the glasses.

—What makes you think he was murdered?

—Sixth sense. Had it coming to him, I'd say.

—Has he been on your mind lately?

Now this really gets to me, it does. This takes the blinking biscuit.

—Me? I've got bugger all in my mind! My mind is a blinking black hole, or trying to be! Then what happens the minute you get a bit of peace, there's all these ruddy people trying to stir things up! Leave me alone!

—Who, Gloria?

—All of you! Piss off! Barging in and filling up my nice empty space, poking your noses into my private beeswax, stirring up all that –

Blimey, there's something violent going on, because he's looking alarmed as hell. It's gone all of a sudden noisy in here, a real rumpus with some old bird shouting her head off. Might be me. And the Jill woman's come back and the teenager's hobbling in on her silly stilts and Mrs Manyon's fussing with a hankie on Dr Kaplan's hand that was clutched in my hand till they prised it off. And the hankie was white but is going red in blotches.

—Are you all right Doctor? Let me just mop up this bit here –

And it's then I see how it's his hand that's bleeding, where I've dug my nails in and scratched. He's a parasite, a bloodsucker, just like Zedorro. Let him pay for what he wants. Let him pay for what he is stealing. Pay for my flesh and blood with his own, he can.

155

—Don't worry, it's nothing, he says, dabbing with the hankie at the scratches.

—First time she's done that, says Mrs M.

—Not quite, I believe, goes the Jill, all flushed up. —Her daughter-in-law said she attacked the baby once.

Face all grim and stiff with hate, if she hates me so much why does she blinking well come, get rid of her.

—Go away, go on, I tell her. —I don't know who you are and where you've come from but you've no business coming along and disturbing my life and so you can bugger off back to the bottom of the blinking lake with your silly beads.

—Beads? goes the doctor man, and I think: oh bloody hell, did I say that.

—Yes, the beads! goes the Jill woman, all excited. —I told you about the glass beads I have, didn't I, Dr Kaplan? The beads she sent me?

Oh so the two of them are one and the bleeding same now, are they. That's why you never spot them both together.

—I think we'll leave it there for today, he goes. —We don't want to overstretch her. It was a pleasure to meet you, Gloria, in spite of . . . well. And he pats my arm.

—She's paying you, isn't she. From her own pocket. Cos she's stinking rich. She's never had a worry in her life, look at her. All this bollocks about something missing. She don't know nothing about missing stuff. Not the way I do.

—Goodbye, Mrs Taylor, he goes. Goodbye, Gloria. Miss Winstanley.

No one's called me Miss Winstanley in years and it brings back the Great Zedorro as easy as if he's walked in the room. But the Great Zedorro's dead, isn't he, murdered in his bed by a madwoman who wanted stuff back that he'd stolen, sucked out of her like blood from a mop stood against the wall in a little bare room.

—Some progress, I hear him tell the Jill woman. —She definitely knew a couple called Bill and Grace. Are you familiar with the name Zedorro?

But she shakes her head.

SHELLSHOCK

Lilac season. From my bed, you can look out on them lovely frothy flowers bobbing their heads in the breeze. Open the window and you get the smell of them, and sometimes a wasp'll buzz in and out again and sometimes a bee. These is quiet days here on the ward, quiet days which rolls into one. At first I thought my eyes had a problem, but no. The blur's from inside.

I sleep for hours on end or sometimes just stare at the wall and I'm so weak I need the nurse to help me use the lav. I'm not hungry for once in my life, even though there's more to eat here than I've seen all through the war. They tell me I've been ill and I believe them, cos my fanny won't stop bleeding, must be something wrong with my ladies' bits. The man who comes to sit by the bed, he don't wear a white coat but you know he's Authority, he looks familiar, if you were the trusting type you'd probably trust him. His wife, if I ever meet her, she'd be one of them people too.

—You had fever. You nearly died, he said. —We've been taking care of you. The war's over. Did you know that, Gloria?

Later a woman I might know brings me a cup of tea, she's all washed-out, she'd be better with a spot of make-up, she would, but not too much because she's blonde, and us blondes need to watch it, you don't want to look like a Slut Fairy or nothing.

—You're in Fyfield Convalescent Home, she says. —Near Bath.

—Are you the Doctor's wife?

—Yes, she goes. —But he's not a doctor exactly, he's a psychologist. Now drink up, then get some more rest.

She don't want to be here, I can sense it. When she leaves she and her psychologist husband whisper in the corner of the room together. Then she goes, wearing a nice smart coat made of tweed. Apart from her and the nurses, I'm the only female around, the others is men, casualties of war with no memories and mutilations, legs blown off and guts scooped out and what have you. I feel like that. Like I've had something blown off or scooped out.

But no. Look at me: I'm whole.

The Slut Fairy's standing by the bed. Some time's gone missing.

—Hello, Grace, I says. —Hello, Slut Fairy.

—My name's Melanie, Gran.

—Don't call me Gran! No one calls me Gran!

—They do now.

She's wearing make-up just like when she was on stage, with her sequinned outfit, but not done so well this time. In fact she looks no better than she should be.

—Here, I brought you a cup of tea, she goes, plonking it down on the bedside table and sloshing some into the saucer and the table which is made of wood, got a drawer in it for my specs and a glass of water for my teeth, which is not in, which is out, because they has been giving me too much gyp, they need to take notice of things like that, the responsibility isn't Hank's, it's Mrs M's, or maybe the doctor's or the dentist's or the accountant's, maybe the insurance man's, the one who does loss of one arm one leg one shoulder any number of teeth up to four.

And while I am stringing this thought together which is like beads, whitey-pink beads which goes one after another and you can make a circle of them and wear it as a necklace, she has got up and buggered off, but she leaves a ghostiness hovering there, which is where she ends and the Slut Fairy begins, cos to my mind they are beginning to be one and the same person, just like the Jill woman and Marje and that little girl, still lurking behind the curtain somewhere near the fish-tank which has fish from the Philippines in, that the Conchita girl looks at till she cries and –

In times of war you drop your knickers down the back
   of a sofa.
In times of war you do things is best forgotten.
In times of war one Yank –

The men scream in the night, and do filthy swearing. In the day the wireless is tuned to the Home Service in case it brings one of them poor bastards to his senses. But fat chance of that, cos not wanting to be rude or anything, most of them is loonies. There is one here called Ned, he is like Iris, young and missing one arm but also half a leg. He was a Prisoner of War and his hair is white, sticking up from his head, and his eyes are red from staring right ahead not blinking. His mum comes to visit him and cries. He don't know who she is. They have made him a phoney arm he can strap on with a harness round his chest but he don't want to wear it. Same with the leg, he prefers to hop.

—It's only my left arm, he says. —Didn't use it much anyway.

He laughs then, like he's said something funny, and his mum turns away.

The loonies take it in turns to go off with the psychologist man and lie on the couch in his room. Sometimes you'll hear a shout or some screaming, but mostly it's quiet murmurs or just silence. Once when Ned was in there you heard this big scream, it went right through you, made you shudder like chalk on a blackboard. He came out looking more shellshocked than before he went in, but you could tell he was happier, like something was off his chest, and the next day when his mum came he smiled and said hello to her, and she burst into tears. He took her face in his hands and kissed her forehead, and I thought: what a good boy, I would like a son like him one day, I would, if I ever have a baby.

Outside wasn't the same place I remembered neither. I could tell from looking out the window, beyond the lilac and into the street. You'd get swirls of people spilling around on the pavement and from pubs, whistling and yelling at each other, some of them, their faces stretched from the smiling and the grinning because the war was over. Even I smiled, though I felt away from it all, because I was in another place, wasn't I, and some time had gone missing somewhere. And some memories too, but I knew better than to start digging. I had an instinct, and you don't fight those instincts, they're there to protect you. When I get out there will be lots of jokes and lots of food, I thought. And if there ain't no chance of that, I'm staying put.

When I could walk and the bleeding had calmed I wandered slow round the grounds in my nightie and admired the Victory Garden, they had good veg there, used to be a tennis court, the gardener told me. He handed me a fresh carrot he'd just washed with the hose and gave a wink while I crunched it. Which got me wondering how Ron was doing, but in a more woozy don't-matter way than before, cos I must've realised he was back in America, or on his way there.

Beyond the Victory Garden there was a bed with foxgloves and marigolds and roses, and beyond that, the fence that kept the world out and a cluster of willows. Sometimes behind the willows you could see the shine and flash of some water, a huge stretch of lake with mud and weed. But take a proper look and it weren't there. Nothing but a meadow with buttercups. The lake, it was imaginary. It was just your head talking.

Things was still blurry but one thing I did know. There was not going to be a knock at the door, there was not going to suddenly be Ron standing there with his cap off, saying, Hiya, cutie, boy, you look a million dollars. I could say bye-bye to ideas like that.

So I sat back from it all, and some of the others in the convalescent place, they did the same – well, most of them in fact, because shellshock does that to you, you're neither here nor there. I didn't spend no time wondering why I hadn't heard from Marje in so long, or why her letters the last year were so short and not very sweet. She'd lost Bobby. She was all cranked up, wasn't she, lost the run of herself. We'd never been what I'd call close. Or why I was bleeding like I had a monthly that went on and on.

Had we ever been close?

D'you know, there's things have completely slipped my mind since the war.

The psychologist came to me one day when I was in my nightie.

—Grace and I are taking you home, Gloria. I think you're ready for it. Mrs O'Malley has moved out, you'll have the place to yourself.

We went by car, a grey Morris Minor with red leather seats. The man drove and his wife sat in the back with her baby. They'd bought me supplies and we carried them out of the boot and put them on the kitchen table.

163

—We saved your coupons for you, said the man. —Grace and I will stay here for the first night, to settle you in.

—I'll make us high tea, said the woman. —How about that?

They might've been cousins or something, from my mum's side, the ones I'd never met before. The baby they had, it must've been a girl cos it was in frills. The woman looked nervous with it, maybe she couldn't cope. She kept trying to feed it syrup of figs from a spoon, then giving up and ramming a bottle in its mouth.

Unless bowels move regularly your child will be weakly, peevish, dull and stunted.

I took against this baby cos every time it cried my tits tingled and I felt sick.

—Here's your letter, says the man, handing me an envelope that's been opened already, sent from America. Inside is a sheet of paper, all crumpled-looking. Writing on it in capital letters.

I don't read it. I just put it in a box.

I howled all night, they told me later. Which was funny, because in the day I didn't feel a flicker. I was dead, wasn't I. Pretty much dead.

The letter that was in the box, Dr Kaplan's left it lying on the table, and my wedding photo next to it. I hate those capital letters he used when he wrote. It looked so –

Well. Call me a snob, but it shamed me, it did, bad handwriting like that. Don't they have proper schools in America?

—Are you going to read it then? goes Doris.

—Can't find my glasses. Hey, Conchita! Where's Conchita?

The pregnant Welsh one comes up instead.

—I want Conchita.

—Your glasses here, Gloria. I tell Conchita to come when she finish making beds.

—When's it due?

—No baby, says the Welsh one who's a foreigner. —Just put on weight.

—Well, that sounds familiar, I tell her. —You'd best see a doctor, declare it and get the extra rations. You don't want to end up with regrets, walking the streets. I know your game.

But she's slapping cushions, doing her deaf act again.

This letter I pen.

Even fifty years on it's a rubbish letter. Wrote it in a hurry, you can tell. Didn't put the time in. Maybe it was her who dictated it, I wouldn't put it past her, she was always the clever one. He was sorry to tell me in this way, sorry they didn't come and tell me in person, but he was invalided out and sent back home, and Marje –

Fuck Marje.

They both felt real bad. Marje wanted me to know she'd always be my sister. Hoped I would forgive them.

But when love comes along –

I remember that line from somewhere, don't I. Don't tell me. You've got to grab it with both hands and not let go, haven't you.

It's the photo does the talking.

There they are in London just before D-Day, him in his uniform, her in the parachute dress, looking like a couple of bloody film stars. She looks like me. Is that why he's married her? Cos she looks like me? We could be twins, he said.

Look at them. Lipstick on our mother's mouth.

Pish pish. Red lips scarlet woman, one Yank and they're off.

It's not crying that I do. No, I don't cry but there's

a howl that comes up from my belly then. A wolf'd make a noise like that if someone stole its cub. Even though it's coming from me, it scares me cos I have never heard such a noise before, this wolf cry, this cry of someone mad.

Doris is watching me read it, and the little girl from Gadderton.

They don't say nothing.

Bloody hell, I'm thinking. I should never've gone fishing, I blame the fish, a trout it was I think, a whopper with Hallelujah eyes, that lived at the bottom of Gadderton Lake. All the other fish, they were impersonators, this was the real McCoy but he was lurking deep because he had a secret.

And now I am hungry.

—When's tea?

—Five o'clock, same as always, says Doris.

—I could eat a horse! Talking of that, here is a joke for you, Doris, you'll like this one. A horse walks into a bar, and sits down. And the barman says to him, Why the long face?

While Doris is laughing I explain to her that it doesn't have to be a horse. It can be an anteater if you want. Any animal with a long face will do.

—We have some papers for you to sign, Mr Authority says the next day. —It's all quite official.

The woman held them out for me and showed me where to put my name. I signed where she said. Didn't bother reading it. Then she left and the baby left with her and I was glad to see the back of them because that baby did bad things to my tits.

—D'you think you'll hear more from Ron? goes the man, whose name is Bill.

—Why would I?

—And your sister?

—Dead. Pretty much dead.

He shook his head and sighed. But he seemed to like the idea.

I didn't mind so much either. It's funny the way I didn't care about neither of them no more. They felt like a couple of foreigners I never really knew.

As soon as I was well enough the man and the woman – they were called Bill and Grace, I think they were my mum's cousins – they gave me some money and I went to live in lodgings in London they'd arranged. It didn't cross my mind to say no, because I'd always wanted to go back and live in the Big Smoke, and I was ready to be somewhere that weren't Bristol.

I was still feeling shellshocked. But it weren't such a bad feeling. In fact it was like a soft cushion, I knew I could come to no harm. I wasn't the only one in a strange mood after the war. You never know how a war's going to hit you, but you know what? Lots of people said afterwards it was the best time of their life, the only time they really felt alive and I know about that because I felt it too.

I stayed in a house in Tooting, right next to one that had been hit in a raid, where the whole family was killed. They hadn't got to their bomb shelter in time. The others, they told me they spent three days trying to dig out any survivors. But there weren't none, just someone's foot and a bit of leg.

There was rubble everywhere, and when the rubble was cleared away there were big empty spaces with puddles in, and pregnant women sprouting up like mushrooms in a field.

Then a few months later, babies and prams. Everywhere you looked there was a baby in a pram. I didn't have no baby in a pram. Never wanted one, did I. Some of them babies didn't have dads, cos the dad was dead or missing or gone back to America. At least I'd been spared that, eh.

Bill and Grace Farraday sent me money once a week, and Grace sent me a picture of herself with her baby girl, wearing its frills. It looked *weakly, peevish, dull and stunted*. I never asked its name, but I sent it some glass beads on a string, what I found on an old bomb-site on Southey Road, where the school had stood that was bombed to bits. They were too good to chuck away. They must've belonged to one of the children. Funny the things that survive in the rubble. Just some old glass beads on a frayed old string, in among the twisted metal and the flapping bits of paper.

I sent the string of beads for Grace's baby, but we lost touch after that. I stopped writing, and the letters stopped coming, and so did the money. But by then I was making my own, wasn't I. Living in Tooting, leading the independent life. Doing all sorts.

—What do you remember? goes Dr Kaplan.

—Nothing. Just . . . nothing. Like I ate a black hole or something.

—Ate a black hole?

—All up. Or it ate me.

—And why do you think you feel like that?

—You're the doctor.

—I'm asking you.

—Listen, sonny Jim. I don't even remember why I don't remember, there's stuff I don't remember forgetting either. If that's any help. I know the Jill woman doesn't believe me and I know Hank doesn't, but it's true. You don't neither, I expect, cos you're on their side.

—But I do believe you, Gloria. I do.

—Crap!

But when I look up to see if he's lying, I find out he isn't. Look at his eyes, his Jew eyes: he ain't kidding me here. You can tell he actually-factually means it. Blinking hell. So I soften a bit, don't I.

—So if you do, why don't they?

—Don't worry about them for now, Gloria. Just settle down for me, for now, OK? Look, it's locked away in your head. The whole story. You just can't reach it, that's all.

—Why not?

—Because you've suppressed it.

—So what do I do?

—We. What we do, Gloria, is that with your permission, we try to bring it back.

Don't like the sound of that, do I.

—What for?

—Not what for, says the Jill woman, walking in and closing the door. —Not what, who. Me, that's who, Gloria. Bring it back for me.

—She's right, says Doris who has slipped in with her and the little girl from the lake trailing drips of weed and mud. —You owe it to her.

Don't blinking well see why, I'm thinking, but I can sense Doris getting ready to give me a rocket, and Dr K is looking hard into my eyes with his Jew eyes, dark and sparkling, and the Jill woman is just waiting. Waiting for her rightful property what is stuck inside me like a baby waiting to be born.

—How?

—The same way you lost it.

—And how was that?

—You know, Gloria, goes Dr K. —You remember that.

And he is right, I do. Oh bugger this for a game of soldiers.

—Will it hurt?

—No, says the Jill woman quickly. —We can promise that.

—We can, says Dr K. —I won't allow anything bad to
happen. And you'll feel better afterwards, he goes. —Don't
be afraid. When you're in the hypnotic state, you'll be able
to recall the memory. You can make your peace with it.
Then if you want, you can let it go again.

—Promise?

—I promise. Close your eyes, Gloria. I want some
shallow breathing. Gentle breathing, in and out.

This is a bit of *déjà* bloody *vu*, this is.

—Is she staying?

—May I? goes the Jill woman.

—If you keep your mouth shut and leave me bloody
well alone, I go.

—Thank you, she says. —All right with you, Dr Kaplan?

—Are you sure it's what you want?

And she nods yes so we are stuck with her.

—Now, Gloria, I want you to settle down on the bed,
put your feet up. Can you do that for me?

So that's what I do and it is a blinking relief to shut
my eyes and not see that Jill face on me that looks so like
Marje, I can tell you.

—Let your body relax completely. I want you to
remember what happened when you had your baby.
You won't feel any of the pain, I promise. You'll just
watch the whole thing from outside yourself. Are you
there, Gloria?

—I'm somewhere.

And I am, I have slid there smooth as warm chocolate.

—What can you see?

—Bugger all.

—Just breathe some more. Don't resist it. I want you to
remember that day. It was the same day the war ended,

Gloria. Where were you? Where were you when you heard about the war ending?

—Leavesden Avenue.

—Can you see yourself now, Gloria?

—Yes, young.

—In Leavesden Avenue?

—Yes. Their house.

—What are you doing?

—Crawling.

—Where?

—Out of the living-room. Into the kitchen. Hands and knees. Dragging two cushions. Got an envelope in my hand.

—Why are you crawling?

—I want to be in the kitchen. For water maybe. I'm on the floor. There's a mop.

I can see it very clearly, this mop. It's leaned against the wall. I'm down on the floor pulling the cushions about so they're under me. Clutching my belly to stop the pain, but it don't work because I am screaming.

—You don't feel the pain, says his voice. —You're just watching.

This girl who is me, she's got no friends, no mum or dad or sister, where is the man that got her here?

—Are you alone?

—Yes.

—And what's happening, Gloria?

—I'm screaming my head off.

—Why?

—Cos I've read the letter and seen the photo. So it's official.

—Are you having the baby, Gloria?

—I can't walk, I want to get out of the kitchen, I don't know what I'm doing there. I'm ripping my dress off cos it's in the way. There's water on the floor. I'm yelling. I'm pushing. The mop's got germs in.

—Take it easy, Gloria. Stand right back from it. Breathe slowly . . . What now?

—Still screaming and pushing. I've rolled on to my back and I'm pushing it out, but it won't come, it's stuck.

—OK, Gloria, keep nice and calm and relaxed. We'll leave out the rest of the pushing, we'll go to the time the baby's born. Can you see it being born?

I am in her body now, doing it, pushing the thing out. No pain but the feelings, they're choking me. And then I see it, I see what I am pushing out from my fanny.

—This thing. Oh Christ, oh damn and blast, it's alive.

—Where is it?

It is out now, first the head and then the shoulders.

—On the floor between my legs.

—What's it doing?

—Crying.

—Why?

—Cos it's a girl.

And now I'm pushing again and it hurts like hell and out comes some liver on a string, with the other end attached to the baby.

—And what are you thinking, Gloria?

—She looks like Marje. Kill her. Strangle her like a chicken or a rabbit. Do it now while she's hardly lived, then it won't count as no crime, just more like an accident. Longer you leave it, worse it'll be. So I'm holding the cord and picking up the little Marje baby. I don't love it, you know. How could I love it when I know what Ron's been up to with my sister? When I've known all along? The photo lying there. Look at them. Look at her in her silk parachute dress she made for Bobby.

—So what are you doing?

—Putting the cord round the baby's neck but it keeps slipping. I'm trying to strangle it. But it's all slippery. It's like a fish.

—And now?

—There's people coming. Someone calling me. Got to finish it quickly. I've got the cord round its neck and my hand over its mouth to stop the crying, and I'm yanking at the cord. And the crying's stopped and the baby has gone blue.

—Is it dead?

—Yes. The baby's dead. It's blue. It's stopped crying.

And good riddance to bad rubbish. When you strangle a small creature such as a rabbit or a baby with its own cord, it's like God's given you the murder weapon. He meant for it to happen, if you believe in Him, which I don't, but I do believe in nature. Tools for the job. What else is it for. The means of giving life also being the means of snatching it off, stands to reason, easy-peasy lemon squeezie. Easy-peasy lemon –

Slippery as a fish, and blood on it, mother's blood. The cord is blue, they don't tell you it's going to be blue or rather mauvey-purple, and that the small creature such as a rabbit or a baby, it'll turn blue too. Or rather mauvey-purple. And the room will go black afterwards, and very quiet.

They don't tell you anything. Which is a crime in itself.

—You see, says Doris. You are doing the right thing and when it is over you will feel a lightness and you will be allowed to go, Glor. That's how it happens. Not to everyone but you are lucky.

Lucky? That must be the worst joke I ever heard.

—Gloria? Can you hear me? says a man's voice through the warm chocolate feeling.

—Just.

—Are you still there? What's happening now?

I look about. The kitchen floor, the mop, the swirl of blood, the small hump of flesh that is my flesh, my flesh and blood. Shouting, and two people bursting in.

—Oh bugger it, the man's there. And so's she. Zedorro's got the baby and he's slapping at it, and the Slut Fairy has got me and she's holding my shoulders and screaming at me.

—Dead, says Zedorro. —I'm afraid it's dead.

—What do we do? says the Slut Fairy. —Did she . . . ?

And they look at me, full of hate.

I must've passed out or something because when I wake up he's doing things. He's taken a big scrap of sheet from the cupboard, looks like Marje's wedding dress but it can't be cos that's in America, ain't it. And he's wrapping the hump of flesh in it.

—And what are you doing now, Gloria?

—I'm lying there thinking: I did one good deed today.

And the man's gone white and his lips are thin and he's holding the bundle and he's saying —Do you realise what you've done, Gloria?

—Let me see it, I go. —I've never seen a newborn baby before, or a dead one for that matter.

He goes and gets the wrapped-up thing. Opens it up, and there's its face.

—Happy? Happy with what you've done?

It's Marje all right.

And yes, I am happy, as a matter of fact. But not for long. Because all of a sudden I am getting another huge almighty whoosh of pain, and I'm screaming again, screaming to high heaven.

This isn't fair.

It was s'posed to be over.

Along the street she wheels a perambulator,
She wheels it in the springtime and in the month of May,

174

And if you ask her why the hell she wheels it,
She wheels it for a soldier who is far, far away,
Far away, far away, far away, far away.
She wheels it for a soldier who is far, far away.

—This is killing you, says Doris.

—Like you said. Don't worry, Doris. I knew. Don't want no more, I don't, I had enough.

—You sure, Glor?

—Yes, sure as eggs. That's me done.

The girl from Gadderton is watching us, bleeding away behind the curtain.

Jill is sitting there crying and rocking in her chair, arms wrapped round herself like she is her own baby.

—It's what they want, I tell her. —It's what she wants, Jill and the little girl with the beads. She wants revenge cos she looked like Marje and I –

Well.

Doris don't say anything.

—And then? goes a man's voice. —What happened after that, Gloria?

The Slut Fairy, she was grabbing Zedorro's arm. Shaking him.

—My God, she says to him. —Look.

—What? he goes.

And I see them both staring at me.

—It's happening again, I go. I need to push.

Above the shelf her father keeps a shotgun,
He keeps it in the springtime and in the month of May,
And if you ask him why the hell he keeps it,
He keeps it for a soldier who is far, far away.
Far away, far away, far away,
He keeps it for a soldier who is far, far away.

Oh Jesus, damn and blast, what is this nightmare. I turn my head away, and heave down like I am shitting, and force the little horror out of me.

Jesus fucking Christ. I have all the bloody luck, I do.

There is no way I am looking at this second damn thing or the afterbirth neither.

When it's all over I watch from the corner of my eye as the Slut Fairy tears up more of the sheet and picks up the second bundle that's alive and hugs it to her and starts snivelling, and the bundle cries, and they've all forgotten I'm there, haven't they, they're so happy, with their little bundle of afterbirth rubbish.

—She knew there was something missing, see, says Doris.

We are looking at the Jill woman who is still hugging herself like her own baby and rocking, rocking. Don't make no noise though cos she has class, don't she, Lady Muck. She looks up, her eyes are red, they are streaming like it is hay fever but no, it's grief. She looks so like Marje after Bobby died, when I found her crumpled up on the floor with the sewing all around her.

—It's what I knew inside me all along, she says. —I knew that the missing thing, it was more a part of me than a mother or a father or a brother.

And she starts her rocking again.

There is a long silence that is screaming out to be filled and it is me meant to fill it.

Doris knows too because she says. —Say it now. Say it to her now, Glor.

Even if it kills me, which it will. So here it comes. The words they're wanting.

—Sorry. I am sorry.

No answer. Silence. She just rocks and rocks in her chair. Not enough.

—You've got to mean it, says Doris. —Do you mean it, Glor?

Well, it hurts so probably I do.

—I took a bit of you away, I go to Jill. —And I took all of her away. I am sorry to her and I am sorry to you.

Did I say it aloud in words or did I just think it?

—Forgive me, then?

I said that.

—It's not so bad here, says Doris. —It's this green underwater feeling. The sky's always blue and you can sleep all the time if you feel like it. Or pay people visits, see how they're doing. It's like a slow green underwater forgetting feeling. Like a dream. You would like it here, Gloria. You can come along any time. Just say the word.

A black hole in space, it's never been properly understood, said a man on the telly. It don't make proper sense. It holds more than it is, it takes up more space than anything but it can be tiny as a golf-ball. The most powerful golf-ball in the universe, the most powerful and the most dangerous and the most hungry, but you wouldn't know nothing to look at it, because when you do, it practically ain't there. It's just like any other ordinary-looking bit of space. Bit darker at the edges, is all. You have to be an expert to spot one. You and me, if we tried spotting one, we'd get nowhere. We'd be looking for a needle in a haystack. In the dark.

So there are Zedorro and the Slut Fairy, fussing over their crying little piece of rubbish and washing the blood and gore off it and ignoring me, and I'm thinking: oh no you don't. You don't leave me here like this with what I have done.

That's when the idea comes. Funny, but this idea I'm

having, it's almost like the little rubbish afterbirth has come up with it, not me.

—There's a way of fixing this, I tell Zedorro. —For me, for everyone.

I'll stop this in its tracks, I will, is what I am thinking.

So with the cold part of my head, I tell him what I want.

—I can't, he says, when I've explained, which don't take long because it's as simple as anything.

—You've got to, I tell him. —You have the power. I've got the want. So do it.

Zedorro looks at the Slut Fairy. The Slut Fairy looks at him, and they have a conversation with their eyes. She holds the little snuffling bundle to her chest and then finally she gives a nod that says, Right, if that's what the price is, yes, but I don't like it.

And turns her back and walks out.

—OK, I'll do it, Gloria, he says. —But you must know that these things aren't done lightly. Best to wait a week or two, settle into it. There are risks. You might find that later on –

—No. Now.

He sighs, looks a bit frantic, like he's wrestling with something. The clock ticks.

—Look, just do it, I tell him. —Just do it now, and you can keep it.

He mumbles something.

—She's right, your wife. It's the price you have to pay. She knows that.

Another long silence with the clock ticking on the wall, ticking away the minutes since death and birth. The two of them never even met, I'm thinking. That is a tidy way of doing it.

—Now or never, I tell him slowly. Because I know that

a little bit of power is mine. —Think about what happens if it's never.

He thinks. Don't like it. But sees my point, don't he, he ain't stupid.

—I said you can keep it, I go. —If you do it now. If you don't, maybe I won't be so sure.

There is a long stretch of time. I shut my eyes and breathe. Then he speaks.

—Not 'it'. He says it softly. —Not 'it'. Her.

Hypnotism works like this. You get a man, it is usually a man, who has a way of looking into your eyes that reaches right clear to your soul. He tells you to do a thing you want to do anyway. You do it.

And when it's done, who takes the blame?

Him?

You?

The war?

No one?

Just him and me now. Me and Zedorro and a little bundle of flesh-rubbish lost in time. All the time in the world we have, it feels like. That's how relaxed he's got me, it is magic, it is a blessed feeling washing over me, warm chocolate, because soon I can be free again, I can feel the empty feeling I am searching for coming towards me.

We are not up there on the stage no more and there is going to be no sawing in half and no bowl of oranges and no rod of steel. His brown eyes look into me like two pools. We have all the time in the world to do what we are going to do.

But it don't take long. In the end it don't take no time really. The results go on and on but what you do, the act itself, it's nothing, it's a relief, it takes a minute only or perhaps a second.

—I want you to close your eyes and imagine a stretch of water, Gloria. A big clear lake, that's very deep. Can you see it?

—Yes.

—I want you to go in. You won't feel the cold. Take the bundle in your arms, and walk into the water as far as you can go.

And so I do, because like the last time, his plan, it don't seem so unreasonable.

—The bundle is heavy, Gloria, because you have weighed it down with stones. Can you feel its weight?

And yes, course I can, it weighs a bloody ton all of a sudden, but before it was just like the weight of a cat or a big rabbit. The bundle is some flesh-rubbish or some flesh and some stones, heavy stones, and the wrapping is like the parachute silk of Marje's wedding dress. I am staggering with how heavy it is, but not scared, not going to fall. I am up to my waist and then my neck.

—Go deeper, Gloria, keep walking, he says. —Go right in and keep going.

And so I do, because I know what we are going to do. It is greeny and silver and underwatery and I keep going, there is no danger, only safety here, me and my bundle walking to the middle of the lake where there are dark weeds and the mud is thick and sleepy on the bottom.

—Now, Gloria. Do it.

So I do. That's where I put it down, with its heavy stones all wrapped in Marje's dress.

And right away the weight is gone and I am free.

—She'll stay at the bottom of the lake, Gloria. She'll stay where you put her because she's weighed down with stones, and when something's weighed down like that, it doesn't resurface. Ever. It will stay there, Gloria, and you will come back, leaving it behind.

—You can come back now, Gloria. You can come back.

And so I shut my eyes and look up through the silver water at the sun and I swim up, up, up through the green forgiving water until I am back in myself.

I MUST'VE SLEPT

I must've slept.

When I open my eyes, Zedorro has gone and Dr Kaplan is sitting there with his notes, and the Jill Farraday woman is rocking like she is her own baby and Melanie is hugging her too so it's a muddle to look at.

—Have I missed something? I go. Because I'd like to've known what got her in that state, I have never seen her show no emotion before to speak of except when she called me a liar and ran out that time with her scarf flying like a flag.

She pushes Melanie off and collects herself, she is good at that. Red red eyes, she's got, and she's fiddling in her handbag for something. Fiddle faddle she goes, till suddenly she finds what she's looking for and fishes out these little glass beads look right familiar.

—My beads, she says. —My glass beads. My mother sent them to me. I mean you did.

—Am I dead yet? I ask them. —Am I in hell?

—No, says Hank. —You're not in hell, Mum. You're here with us.

—Then take me to that place we caught a fish. Take me to Gadderton. Gadderton Lake. Doris is waiting for me.

They look at each other.

—When you're feeling more yourself.

Myself? What is that? I have stopped knowing.

—Did it hurt? asks Dr Kaplan.

—Did what hurt? I was asleep. I had this dream.

He looks anxious.

—What did you dream?

—I remembered what Zedorro did. In the war.

They're shooting looks at each other, worried that perhaps I am nuts.

—The hospital they put me in with shellshock, that's where he worked. For the MOD. He worked with the ones who'd got amnesia, helping them remember stuff. But he did other memory things too. There were these soldiers who saw things that was so bad they went mad with it. There was one called Ned.

—Ned? goes Jill, with her crying-wobble voice. —Ned Sullivan? I knew him! Uncle Ned, he was one of Dad's patients, he'd lost an arm and part of one leg –

—That's the one.

—He used to come to the house, he used to talk with Dad for hours. Dad always called him his 'guinea-pig'. But I never knew why.

—Cos he treated him. And he must've been the first. For the new treatment.

—What did he do? asks Dr Kaplan, all excited. —What was this treatment?

—It was supposed to be secret, but Ned talked about it and so did some of the others. They all wanted to have the treatment. Ned was the first.

—What did it involve? goes Dr K. —What happened to you if you were part of it?

—I remember them going in mad and coming out happy, I go. They're all listening to me now, and Dr K is even getting out his pen and paper. —That's what I remember about them days in the hospital. Didn't always work though. Some of them went in mad and came out just

184

as mad. Or they went in mad and came out happy, then a week or two later they were screaming again. Cos the treatment didn't always work, see. Ned, he was the first and he was a big success.

Jill makes a noise.

—No he wasn't.

Dr K is scribbling like mad.

—What? I thought he was.

—He was for quite a few years. Through most of my childhood. Then when I was a teenager – he went strange. It started slowly, then it got worse and worse. Dad couldn't do anything to help him. He tried but it only made it worse. Ned was furious with Dad. Said he'd made his life hell. He died a few years after Dad. In an institution.

—So what was the treatment? goes Dr K. —Can you remember what it was, Gloria? What he did?

—He wiped people's memories. So they'd forget what they'd seen and sometimes –

—What they'd done?

—Yes. Bad stuff. They had to really want to forget it, whatever it was. They had to be nearly going mad with it. They had to sign something, accepting the risk. Cos other things might get wiped with it. They'd talk about how much they wanted it, they was queuing up to have it done on them.

The Jill woman, she's got her hands clasped together and she's back to rocking back and forth, back and forth.

—You look like you've seen a ghost, I tell her. —Has someone died?

More photographs of their bloody wedding arrive, forwarded from Bristol. There they are, smiling at me, rubbing the salt right in. The worst thing is what Marje rubs in. Because in every single one of them pictures, she looks just like me.

185

I must've been in a trance, because Hank and Hank's Wife and Jill is suddenly here, and Jill's trying to open my hand that's got the letter scrunched in it, and the toddler has got a plastic trike.

But I'm remembering.

—Please, Mum, goes Hank.

—Please . . . Gloria, goes Jill, prising at my fingers.

I'm remembering how I put that first photo on the mantelpiece in Tooting, and started to wear our mum's old wedding ring. When my men asked me where my husband was – it used to worry them, in case he showed up halfway through a session with a shotgun, I suppose – I said he was dead. That could bring me some warmth. One client of mine, a bloke from Balham with a face like a pimply old lobster, Mr Loomis, he'd get tears in his eyes when he looked at that picture of me in my wedding dress, looking so beautiful.

When actually it was me that was dead, wasn't it, after what they'd done?

A rubbish letter full of crap. Written by a bastard, dictated by a –

There's no word for my sister.

He didn't mean it, of course, about wanting me to visit them in Chicago one day. But he wrote it, didn't he.

—Well, we know who Jill's dad was, says Hank. He and Karen are holding hands and the toddler is whizzing about on his trike. —But who was mine?

FISH AND CHIPS

In my dream I saw the Slut Fairy in the street wheeling a pram. It was springtime, April or in the month of May. We nodded at each other like people in a queue. Funny; I didn't trust myself no more. As in, I didn't know how well I knew her. I still had a spot of shellshock. I remember her in her sequins and her false tits, and now here she was, a flat-chested mother pushing a pram. She could have been me, except I didn't have a baby, did I.

Then I pop awake and for a minute, everything's clear.

—Was she a good mother?

Jilly's eyes is still all red from crying. The others have gone. Dr Kaplan's gone back to London on the train for his Christmas holidays, most likely, buying himself a sandwich from the trolley in the carriage, they do a nice tuna-and-mayonnaise one.

—Yes. She was a good mum. But she died when I was a teenager.

—Oh. That's a shame.

—And then my father – had problems.

When she blows her nose she looks like a little girl, but with Mum's mouth.

—Like what?

—He drank. I never knew he started out as a stage hypnotist. I never knew about the name Zedorro. Our name was Farraday. I thought he was properly trained – but that came later, I suppose. I had no idea till I saw the newspaper cutting of him and my mother doing a show in Bristol.

She pulls it out.

—This one.

—Show it me, I go, and grab. Because immediately it looks familiar.

—I've got that same picture, I go. —In my box.

—Hank gave it to me, she says. —It's my father and mother.

—And me.

—You?

—Her, see? I'm that one, stretched out with the oranges on her tummy. That's me. It's how we met. (You have to squint to see my face, it's just a blur.)

And there I am, with the flash going off that I can feel through my shut eyes, and later I am standing up and they is cheering, cheering, and Ron is out there in the audience and he is just waiting for me to come back and he will say, You sure looked good up there, hon.

I must've slept again. When I wake she is still there, Jill. But crying less.

—Ask her a question, says Doris. —Show some interest in the poor woman. Look at what she's gone through to find you and come here. Takes guts, that does, tracking down your real mum.

All right then.

—And what about your husband? Where's Melanie's dad?

She looks up, shocked I have spoken to her, I s'pose.

—Collins? She spits his surname like it's poison and twists her paper hankie into a little scrunch. —We're

188

divorced. We don't see him. He's a gambler. And a drunk. He lost everything. I don't even know where he is. The Far East somewhere. Propping up a bar. She sniffs and dabs at her lady's nose. —Then I married again but my second husband died.

—Rich, was he?

—Of leukaemia. A few years ago.

So that's why she looks so miserable, in spite of the chequebook. Then I remember the song.

—'Don't Fall in Love with a Gambler', I tell her. Kenny Rogers. You know the song? It is Kenny Rogers, isn't it? Or is it that Willie Nelson one? I get them muddled up.

But she's concentrating hard on her patch of wall.

Hank's holding my hand. We are on the pier again, the seagulls rippling in and out on the wind-gusts. It's chilly and the sky is hanging low. Little plops of rain dropping.

—So you never went to Chicago?

—I'm looking for the one with the stump. The poor old gull with the stump.

I'm chucking them old crumbs from this morning's toast. Bits of the truth, and bits of lies, and all so jumbled up together I don't know no more.

—All that time I was working in London, you know – I couldn't get pregnant, no matter how hard I tried. Didn't get pregnant for ages, did I.

—Mum, he says. —Please. Don't.

—That was fate telling me something.

—Fancy some fish and chips? he says in this loud breezy voice. —Because I could do with some.

And he's off, striding towards the chippie and leaving me there with the crumbs and the seagulls all around.

*   *   *

189

—I've brought the baby oil, I tell old Ed. Cos I want one last Zedorro Moment before I go.

—Zedorro Moment? What's that? And before you go where? You leaving?

—I'm joining Doris. I've had enough. Bags packed and ready.

—Don't talk like that, Gloria. Glorious Gloria. Don't cry, love. Who's been getting at you this time?

—Oh the usual. The grown-ups. Question after bloody question. They can't just let sleeping dogs lie.

—Come on then, he goes, and he pulls me down on the bed.

He's in his dressing gown and jim-jams.

—You know what I wanted, all the time I was earning my living in London, before Hank was born? Hank don't want to hear about it, of course, he'd rather stuff his face with chips.

—What, he goes. While I pour some baby oil on my hands, he's getting out his whatsit for me to see to. I always did like seeing to them things, don't ask me why. Some people just have a taste for it, I s'pose.

—What was you wanting? Ooh, that's chilly. Warm it up first, missis, or you'll turn him into an icicle! You'll turn Grosvenor into a –

—Grosvenor?

—That's his name.

Lord help him.

—I wanted a little babby, I said. —Every time I was with a client, I was hoping I'd fall preggers. Just wanted a little babby to hold. I don't know why. It was like there was this hole in me needed filling.

—I'll find your hole, he says. —I'll fill it.

—You're all talk, I tell him.

But Grosvenor's hardening up.

—I never lost the knack, see, says Ed. —Never lost my

manhood, I didn't. Some of 'em do but not me. Pleased as punch, he is, with his stiffy called Grosvenor.

From my big bed you could see the mantelpiece, with my wedding photo on, and every time I did it with a man I'd think of Ron, saying, Yeah, cutie, yeah that feels good, you sure know how to make a man go crazy, you sexy little cute-assed bitch, driving me wild . . .

Drove me wild, too. And then the feeling got stronger and stronger. It was Ron's baby I was going to have. That's what I wanted. Not just any baby, it had to be Ron's. It was like there was a space inside me, a space where only his baby belonged. And I knew if I imagined Ron, the babby I had would be his. I know it don't make sense. But it did to me.

—I took on more and more clients, I'm telling old Ed. —I was doing it morning, noon and night. I needed untangling by the end of the day, I did!

—Gruh-huh, he goes. —Umph. Pah.

—Made plenty of money but I couldn't get what I wanted.

I'm stroking and yanking away like an old pro while I'm talking, and his old whatsit that's called Grosvenor is standing nicely to attention. Not bad for an old codger with a dicky heart, eh.

—Easy does it, goes Ed. —I'm ninety-one.

—You're a dirty little boy, you are. Anyway you was just boasting about your manhood, you want to make a fuss, I'll stop.

—Nah, keep going, girl. You're a natural, you are. How much did you charge then? In them days?

—Ten shillings. Fifteen, for the American thing. I was good at that.

—I bet you were. You going to show me then, you little prick-tease? I've never had one of them. Heard about them though.

—If you're a good boy. Haven't done it in years, I'll need to take my teeth out.

—There's my girl.

When I've got them out I put them in the jar with his, and they sit there in the Steradent like two pink crabs that's huddled together and has fallen in underwater love.

—I can't talk while I'm doing it, mind, I tell him.

—That's all right, Gloria my Glorious, I'll do the talking.

He doesn't though, he just does the moaning and the groaning and the Oh Gloria, and it makes me squirm with pleasure myself, and soon I'm wanting some of the action too, so I hop on top of him and we're away, just like the old days, it's like rocking in a creaky old rocking chair, his face below me purple and his eyes googling while my tits wobble against his chest.

—Oh Gloria, he's going. —Oh Gloria! You're going to kill me, you are!

Puffing and panting and wheezing away like an old warhorse.

Oh Ron, I'm thinking. Oh Ron.

—*I'm going to marry you, hon. You're coming to Chicago with me.*

And the next thing I know, out of the bloody blinking blue I've had a big wave of it, a big old you know what, a Zedorro Moment or whatever you like to call it, which I haven't had such a good one of in many a long year.

And Ed must've had a bit of a crisis too, cos he's heaving about underneath me, black and blue with it, and panting like mad, and his eyeballs has gone right up in his head. That's my boy.

—That's my boy, I go, stroking his darling old face.

—Don't knock it, I tell Mrs Manyon when they've hauled me off him and covered him up with a sheet. Old people have a right to a sex life just like anyone else. Anyway, he died happy.

But she just throws me this look like I'm scum.

THE WINDY CITY

Conchita la Paz, she likes to look at them fish, because they come from the Philippines, from the rivers and the sea which is bright blue. Happy fish, bright as plastic. Conchita la Paz is sleeping now, because she's not on night-shift, no one is, but Melanie's here, and they're friends, them two, you might not've realised that. I saw them chatting in the Day Room, and they must've thought all the oldies was asleep or dead, because all of a sudden Melanie pulls down her trousers and shows Conchita this tattoo she's got, and Conchita giggles like mad and starts shrieking with laughter. It's a snake, coming out of her bum. Funny what gets some people going, isn't it. But maybe if tattoos were the thing when I was her age, I'd have had one done. Not a snake from the bum but something else. A crab on one of my tits maybe, pretending to pinch a nipple with its claw, in memory of Ron.

The light is off. There is this bit of moonlight.

But mostly we are in the dark, the moonlight is outside, and some light from the street-lamps which is orange. But here is dark, that is a soft dark.

Me and the girl Melanie that calls me Gran. We are sitting in the soft dark and I am thinking of a thing I saw through the window of the hospital. It was this big orange crane. It had a wrecker ball that it swung to make the walls crash down. It swung and it swung, doing its wrecking thing till everything was gone.

The girl doesn't say nothing, she might be asleep, or on drugs, you never know. She had a row with her mum. Her mum has gone off. Her mum don't want to see me no more after what happened to Ed and maybe other reasons too. Stuff that has been lost down the back of the sofa.

A thousand squids you can win if you confess enough stuff on that show.

Just when I was getting used to her, just when she wasn't narking me so much. She went hysterical, called me a murderer. I heard a good joke, Hank told it me. What do you get when you cross a Jehovah's Witness with an Atheist?

Someone who knocks on the door for no reason.

Anyway, here is Melanie next to me in the dark, with her nose-stud and a reptile hid up her bum, wonder if her mum knows. Sitting with me, and the lights is out everywhere, even the light in the fish-tank is out, and just a bit of tinsel glinting on the tree.

Me, watching that wrecking ball in my head. Swinging and swinging.

Along the street she wheels a perambulator,
She wheels it in the springtime and in the month of May,
And if you ask her why the hell she wheels it,
She wheels it for a soldier who is far, far away,
Far away, far away, far away, far away.
She wheels it for a soldier who is far, far away.

My voice sounds like an old lady's voice, not like I thought it would be, I thought I would sound young again. Can't sing that song without remembering what happened to Iris, and the sight of her arm and shoulder and the engagement ring on her finger showing she's a dark horse. Melanie stirs, so I reach out for a knitting needle and stab her arm.

—You got a fella then?

Melanie laughs, sleepy.

—Plenty.

—Marje always used to say you have to grab love where you can and hang on to it. You only live once.

—Got a joke for you, Gran.

—I know it.

—How d'you know you know it?

—Cos I have told you all the jokes, you know I have. Last few days I have done my whole blinking collection for you.

That is true. I have. She likes a joke, this girl, she likes a laugh. Unlike her mum.

—I have told you them all, and you ain't hardly told me a single one I don't know already. So what's it about?

—Alzheimer's.

—See? Told you. Know it, the punchline is, At least I don't have cancer. Been there, done that, little Miss Muffet.

—Different one, she says, you'll see. Ready?

Well, I can't resist a joke, can I.

—Man's worried about his wife so he takes her to the doctor, doctor examines her, says he needs to speak to the husband alone. Says to the husband, Right. The diagnosis is very bad. Your wife has either got Alzheimer's or Aids, and I don't know which. Oh God, says the man. How can I find out? Well, says the doc after he has done a bit of thinking. You take her into the woods and leave her there. And if she makes her way home –

—Don't fuck her!

Knew it, see.

But she is not so bad, this girl what calls me Gran. She

reminds me of someone I knew. Silly girl, bit thick, but not so bad.

It's still dark, but there's the beginning of grey beyond the black. The fish is flitting about, they are grey. In their dark tank. Maybe we slept.

—OK, Gran, she says yawning. —Why don't you just tell me the truth, and get it over with? I mean the whole truth.

—What for? When's the truth ever done anyone any good?

—For Mum's sake. And Hank's. And Calum's. For posterity.

—Posterity? What kind of a word is that?

—It's me. And my kids, if I have them. It's you. It's how you're remembered.

—Is that a fact. And what makes you think I give a monkey's about all that?

—I know you do.

—You know wrong.

—Look. Gran.

—Don't call me that!

—Gloria. Whatever. You're . . . not all bad.

—What are you buttering me up for?

—I meant it. I mean it.

—Like hell.

I pick off this bit of wool from my skirt. It's bluey, sort of mauve, nice colour.

—Certain bits of the past is lost property, I'm afraid, I tell her. —Skedaddled. Missing presumed dead.

She just gives me a look. One of those looks, you know the ones.

—Don't blame me you're here, I tell her. —Blame Mister Hitler. Sex was everywhere. It came with death. And rationing.

And love, I think, but I don't say that. What would she

198

know about love? Love was what you grabbed and hung on to, way past hope, way past reason. Or sometimes it just came zinging at you from nowhere, like a hand grenade someone threw. Bong! And you're a goner, they can scrape you off the floor after that.

—Tell her, says Doris.

Another bit of wool coming loose on this skirt, I need some new clothes, I do, a trip to Marks and Spensive, and suddenly all I want is some peace.

—Go on then, help yourself to my beeswax. Be my bloody guest, young madam. But if you don't like what you hear, don't come crying to me, because where I am, I'm way past caring.

Doris is still there, but fainter now, all underwatery. Just the outline of her, rippling like she's drowned.

—*Tell her what happened*, she says in her little underwater voice. —*Tell her about Hank.*

So I do this big sigh, comes from right deep inside, and I begin.

—I went there in a boat, I tell the Melanie girl. —A ship, more like. The *Liverpool Lady*, it was called. Not that there was any ladies in Liverpool.

She looks puzzled.

—Where did you go?

She is thick and all.

—America! Where else?

I can hear her breath draw in.

—Say that again?

—I went to America. Read my lips.

—But you – I thought you – we thought you –

—Made it up. Didn't you.

I can hear her breathing some more.

—Yes, she goes, her voice a bit shuddery beneath the moon. —We did. We thought you made it up.

199

—It took ten days to get there. Nowadays you hop on a plane and you're there in a flash, aren't you. Well, we had ten days of being seasick and chucking up our dinner.

—But why? Why did you go?

I can't answer that for a minute, and we sit there in the dark for a while, listening to the clock tick.

—Maybe I had this thing driving me.

—What thing? What happened, Gran? What happened?

The clock ticks some more in the dark, and I fall asleep or something, and maybe I dream the rest or maybe I tell her, and as the story rolls on, the light begins to creep in, the darkness is thinning out, turning from black to grey to light grey, and gulls is out there, you can hear them squawking and flying away over the blue skies, smiling at me, blue days all of them gone, nothing but blue skies from now on, what I would do to fly.

What I would do to fly.

It was my Balham client, Mr Loomis, gave me the money. He felt sorry for me, with my only relative being a sister who was abroad, because my mum and dad was dead and so was my husband, all I had in the world was Marje. Mr Loomis was rich, he was in property, he was building London after the bomb damage. Giving it a makeover, so where there was rubble and misery once, there is fresh blocks of flats with spanking new toilets.

—I'm in the business of sweeping the past under the carpet, he says to me. —Where it belongs. I believe in fresh starts, I do. No one wants to remember London like that.

His wife was blown to bits in a raid. He is a good man.

—Just have a nice time, he says, handing me this wad of cash, looks like fivers and tenners, from the colour. —And then come back and tell me all about it. You're a good girl, Gloria. You've given me the best sucking off I ever had and I've had a few in my time, darling. So come on. Accept a talent bonus, sweetheart. I don't like to see you sad.

—Were you scared?

—Course I was. I started regretting it as soon as I got on board the ship, but I can't swim so that was that.

Ten days of chucking up my dinner and crying in the cabin, and when we docked in New York the harbour was steaming and the Statue of Liberty rose up from the water, green as green. Thousands of us came off the gangplank banging suitcases and bags and waited for hours in Immigration till finally we were through to the streets, jam-packed with people – men in suits, men in overalls, old ladies, women with prams, girls with high heels and little swinging handbags.

—What was it like?

—Foreign. Like landing on the moon.

Ron's moon, is what it was. They all spoke like him, he weren't a foreigner here. That night I stayed in a cheap hotel with a girl called Josie I met in the Immigration queue, who came from Hull and had one leg shorter than the other and a special shoe. She'd come to look for her GI in St Louis, she said. He hadn't written but she knew he was alive. I told her I'd come to see my sister because I didn't want to get started on my story, did I. It wouldn't cheer her up none. I didn't sleep a wink because she was crying and there was creepy-crawlies scuffing about with long waving-about feelers and flat brown shells. Next morning we went to a diner and ordered eggs, and the cook said, Sunny-side-up or over-easy? And we laughed, thinking he was taking the mickey till he explained it was two different ways of frying them. Then we went to the Greyhound Bus Station and when the ticket man said, Where to, ladies, she said, St Louis, single, and I said, Chicago. The same.

When we hugged goodbye and said good luck, I thought: poor girl, she is going to need it. And I sat on a bench eating a hot dog while I waited for my bus. It tasted good but I could hardly swallow because of the fear and the wishing I hadn't come and the little voice saying, *Don't go to Chicago, Gloria, let sleeping dogs lie. Go back to London and live your life and let them two live theirs.*

—Are you serious about all this? she goes, opening some gum and popping it in her mouth. I can smell the hot mint of it. —You really went there? You're not just –

—Making it up? Well, yes. Course I am. It's all a load of cobblers and I am telling it you just for the blinking fun of it because old folks gets bored stuck in Homes with only tropical fish and half-dead people to look at. Silly cow.

—Sorry, Gran.

—Should think so too. If Ed was alive I know what I'd be doing now, and it don't involve raking over the past, that's for sure.

She chews some more and sighs.

—So you went to Chicago.

The yellow cab stopped by a little wooden house. A shack, it was, somewhere on the outskirts of the city, nowhere near the middle like I'd hoped. Hadn't known what to expect but it wasn't this. I knew it was the right place because of the Dynamo petrol station next to it, Ron's dad's petrol station where Ron's dad worked and Ron used to work too. The house, it was a rectangle, reminded you of a big matchbox. Not a pretty one neither, just a very ordinary one. *Chicago.* When he first said Chicago, it sounded like the flicks, it sounded like gold, but now I

202

can see it is just a place where plain people live and have fights like anywhere else.

So this is where she's ended up, I think, dragging my suitcase into the porch. Well. No great shakes.

That makes me feel better, gives me the courage to ring the bell. Then once I've rung it I start trembling like a leaf of course, hoping she's out, hoping she's in, hoping for Ron and not her to be there so we can be the two of us alone, hoping for I don't know what cos I am that mixed-up in myself. Heart pounding.

Door opens, and it's her.

Good old betraying two-faced Marje.

She still looks just like me – that's my first thought. *My face, but not as pretty, and our Mum's mouth. I should've had that mouth, she don't deserve it. She don't deserve nothing.*

—Gloria! she goes, in this whisper, so small you can't hardly hear it. Her whole face slumps, caves in, like I've whacked her full on with my fist. —My God. What are you doing here? Her voice has gone a bit American.

—Pleased to see me, are you? I go. I'm whispering too, and gulping back this big gulp.

We stand there for a long time just looking. Her at me, and me at her, like one person looking at themselves in the mirror, because I can feel my face slumping too, and feel the same bad things she's feeling welling up wild and hot like blood from a gash. Then again like someone in a mirror, our faces twist at the same time, and we both start crying and throw ourselves into each other's arms, hitting each other one minute, hugging each other the next, hitting, hugging, kissing, wanting to scratch and bite like two dogs fighting or mating. On and on, and we're screaming stuff too, and choking on the words, don't know what we're screaming exactly but it ain't pretty, oh no not nice at all, it is cruel things that comes from hate, the kind of hate you get at home, from people you loved.

And after a bit of this we both stumble to the floor, howling and howling and hugging and howling, the two of us in the hallway with the door wide open for all to see.

And then in he comes, must be from the garage next door, yelling.

—What the heck? And he drags us both inside, saying what the hell's going on here, can someone please explain what the fuck's going on, Jesus fuckin' Christ, Gloria, Marje, Gloria, Gloria, oh Gloria, oh Marje.

But he wasn't part of what was going on there. It was between me and Marje.

It didn't stay that way, of course.

He was not happy to see me, not one bit. Nor was she. Worst thing that could have happened, I was. But a while later, after we'd all calmed down a bit and Marje and I had stopped crying, I went to their bathroom for a wash and brush-up, and while I was in there they must've had a talk, because after that they did a good job of pretending.

In the kitchen they have a thing called an ice-box.

He goes and gets out three root beers and opens them. We swig straight from the bottle till it makes me queasy.

—I was invalided out, see, Gloria, says Ron. —That's why I came back early.

—We got married as soon as he was out of hospital, goes Marje. —Got permission from his CO, and came straight here.

They are both speaking fast, like they have agreed to tell me what wasn't in the letter, get it over with, all the gory details.

—I crashed the plane coming home after a mission.

Just after D-Day. Both wings were hit and I was lucky to get her home at all. I still don't know how the fuck I got out of the wreck, I had concussion real bad, lost my balance. That's why they sent me back, doc said it could come again any time. My head still ain't right.

—Yes. He gets depressed and aggressive, says Marje. Bitter, she sounds. —Don't you, Ron?

—Yeah, he goes. —Depressed, mostly. But sometimes aggressive too, yeah.

—What year was this? asks the slutty one. —That you went to America?

—Oh. 1946, I think. The date was round about June 17, 1946.

—How long did you stay?

—Oh. Only a few minutes.

There's a patch of silence and the moonlight glows like radiation.

—America's a long way to go just for a few minutes, she says.

—It may've been longer. I can't remember. A week, perhaps. A month.

—A year?

—No, definitely not a year. Just a few minutes. That's what it seemed like.

—So now you're here, says Marje, her face creaking with brightness, we'll make the most of it. I'll show you round town. Oh, there's so much to see! We can all go to a baseball game. She can meet some of our friends, can't she, Ron? I bet Izzi would like her – didn't you say he was coming over from New York next weekend?

Her voice is all breakable, she is all breakable, she is like glass, and glass is scared of being smashed and she knows me, she knows I can be someone that smashes.

So watch out, Marje. Marje, who, the very first time she met him, went and put on lipstick pretending it was for sending lipstick kisses in a letter to Bobby. But that was bollocks, the lipstick was for Ron and she'd made her mind up then and there that she was going to have him, and Bobby being killed was a blessing for her.

Marje had a job. Nursing. She was trained now, she worked in this hospital in the city, took the tram there. Chicago. It used to sound like the flicks. But real life's never the same, is it. I didn't see much of it, but I saw enough to know it wasn't like I thought. But then nothing is. The women, they all wore flowers in their hair, it was the fashion that summer, and they dressed in bright colours, with little jackets and sleeveless dresses. And the toilet paper! It wasn't like Bronco, it was soft, it was a pleasure to wipe your arse with it.

As for Marje – oh, quite the happy wife, she was, on the surface. But you could tell something was wrong, and I began to wonder how long it would be before the cracks started to show, because Marje is someone always wants what she don't have, but with marriage you've made your choice, haven't you, and you don't move on after that. That's the thing she couldn't see yet, but I could, I knew her. Her mouth, it turned down at the sides more than it turned up. Her mouth gave things away that the rest of her didn't.

I knew the time would come when I'd be alone with Ron. From the minute I saw him, and this look went between us, I knew.

Marje knew too of course, because she wasn't stupid. I was the stupid one, remember.

Ron is working in his dad's garage, and me and Marje are on the verandah, it is a sweltering day. The cars drive by flashing in the sun, Louis Armstrong is on the radio.

You could be happy here if you didn't have things on your mind. Things such as, your sister nicked your man.

—Remember the day I first introduced you to Ron?

She looks away.

—Not really, she says. —Can't say I do.

—He came to the house, to take me on a date. He brought a tin of peaches.

—Canned peaches? You can buy them any day here. Just stroll down to the grocery store, pay a dollar, they're yours.

—It was the same day Iris got her arm blown off. Remember that? I ask her.

—What? she goes, looking shocked. —Iris? You're kidding! Was I there?

—No, you were wearing orange, so you'd done the night-shift. But you heard it, you heard the bang.

—Did I? I can't remember. What happened to her? How is she?

—Dead. I wrote to you. She topped herself.

—You never.

—I did. You losing your memory or what?

She looks blank for a minute and then she laughs.

—Must be. Because I'm happy. I forget all the bad times. It all seems so long ago, the war. Best forgotten anyway.

You know what this is all about. She is forgetting stuff on purpose, she is. Forgetting Ron's first visit, forgetting the bang she heard when Iris was blown up, and very soon of course she will forget that Ron was my boyfriend before she nicked him. She will start to believe that he was hers right from the start, and maybe even that there was no Bobby.

—Are you still in touch with Bobby's mum? I ask.

Because I'm curious, now that I'm getting this idea about Marje's memory.

—No, she says. —Didn't seem no point. I'm in America now. Bobby's dead. I won't be going back. You have to leave the past behind, you know. She pulls down her sunglasses and looks out into the street. —Hot day. Never got this hot in England, did it?

—Sometimes you can't leave the past behind though, can you, I say. —Sometimes it takes a boat and then a bus and then a cab and it knocks on your door, don't it, Marje?

—Yes, she says. —It sometimes does. (Voice all weak and faint.) —Fancy another beer? she says, getting up all of a sudden and smoothing her frock. —I'm that parched.

She is gone a long time, and when she comes back with the two bottles from the ice-box she looks shaky and has put on more lipstick.

—You have to look to the future now, Gloria, she says. —Find yourself a man. There's a friend of Ron's called Izzi, he's coming soon. You'll like him, he has some stories to tell.

I don't say nothing, so she gets out two Lucky Strikes from a pack and hands me one.

—It's a good life here. I wouldn't go back to England for the world. I've turned my back on it, I have. Nothing left for me there.

—Except family, I say.

—Well of course, she goes quickly. —I didn't mean it like that. We take a few drags and then she can sense me about to ask her more stuff so she laughs quickly and says —They've got these things called tea-bags. First time I had a cup of tea in a lunch-room, they gave some hot water and one of these bags. I just ripped the bag open to get the tea out.

I don't say nothing so she laughs again and then starts singing, low.

Smoke smoke smoke that cigarette.
Puff puff puff and if you smoke yourself to death,
Tell Saint Peter at the Golden Gate that you hates to
   make him wait . . .

She wants me to join in, like in the good old days, but I am not giving her that pleasure so she has to finish the chorus all alone in her cracked-up voice.
You gotta have another cigarette . . .
I have never seen my sister so unhappy.

After that little talk she knew it was war, a different kind of war than the one we'd lived through in England, a worse kind of war, a female one where another woman's the enemy. She started guarding him like a hawk, always one hand on him somewhere – on his arm, touching his knee if they were sitting, or just a finger sometimes smoothing a collar or flicking off an invisible speck. Her hands all over him, showing me he was hers, see. Property of. Still had that mouth. Our mum's mouth. But harder now, less pouty. You could see in a few years it would start to sag at the sides with this disappointment she was beginning to learn all about, that she always had brewing in her because she always wanted the thing she didn't have.

Me? I'd learned it already, hadn't I.

Learned the worst, had a small taste of the best, even though it was only a joke as it turned out, and a bit of a sick one, a bit of a dirty one.

Hang on to love, I used to think.

Now I thought: it's not love you grab, it's any kind of a future, any kind you can make out of what's left of yourself.

And him? The great movie-star, Mr GI Joe, one Yank and they're off? Mr Oversexed, Overpaid and Over Here?

Well. It wasn't about love, was it. Not any more. We were beyond that now, weren't we.

Marje wouldn't rest till we had all got together and met Izzi. Izzi, he was an Italian American, and he was famous because he and some others survived eighty-three days on a raft in the ocean after their ship was torpedoed. He was going round the whole of America giving public talks about it, and that's why he was in Chicago. He and Ron knew each other because they were Ninety-Day Wonders together when they enlisted. We took a cab to a bar with pinball machines and flashing lights, and soon we were halfway to being blotto, the four of us, because there was that much tension between me and Marje and Ron.

He was good to look at, Izzi. And I flirted with him of course, but only to see what it would do to Ron. The more he talked about the raft, the more I flirted, but discreet-like, just enough for Marje to think I fancied him and Ron to notice. There were seven to begin with on that raft. They lived on some rations at first, till they ran out and they had to trap rainwater and kill fish and birds using their bare hands, or spears made of scissors.

—Things just went from like bad to very bad, real quick, says Izzi. —We had two knives to start with, but we lost both of 'em in no time. One got knocked off the side when we was catching a fish, the other one . . .

As he talked I slid closer to him on the seat, and Ron frowned. He wasn't happy about it, but what could he do? He was a married man, he'd made his bed, and he'd have to lie in it. But the thing about that bed was, I had a feeling it wasn't as hot as it once was. *Depressed and aggressive*, Marje said. Can concussion do that to you? Maybe it can, but so can other stuff.

Izzi was still talking about his friend.

—First he went deaf, then he went blind. We had no

protection from the sun, and we weren't eating practically nothing. And then he got this like, paranoia? He thought we were all hiding the fresh water from him. But there wasn't no fresh water. We were all just lying there half dead, waiting for the rain with our mouths hanging open. And in the morning he was dead.

Marje slaps her hand over her mouth.

—He wasn't, she goes.

—Let the guy talk, goes Ron. He gives her a look that I wouldn't like to get if it was me, a look that says, You silly cow.

—He sure was, goes Izzi. And he wasn't the only one. (I slide even closer to Izzi.) —We pushed him off the raft and watched him sink down. Jeez, that was a sight. His hair kinda floating behind him as he went down, it made you realise he was going somewhere peaceful. After that we kept talking about what food we'd eat when we got ashore. What meals we'd have.

Banana custard, I'm thinking. Steak-and-kidney pie. Jam roly-poly.

—I'd have spaghetti bolognese, says Marje out loud, and Ron gives her another bad look, and she takes a big swig of her drink and flashes him an angry look back.

—Then we all started having these hallucinations, goes Izzi. —I kept thinking we were next to land, and all I had to do was swim to it. Then I kept seeing a lunch-room. Kept wanting to walk in there and order everything on the fuckin' menu.

Ron's looking at me watching Izzi, I can feel his eyes on me. So I keep smiling harder and harder at Izzi, encouraging his story along, which is now about how this man Maddox who was on board, his hallucinations were so good that when he talked about them, the others started believing in them too.

—He saw like these mountains of hamburgers. Hershey

211

bars. And he saw his cute wife, and he saw chocolate cake and he saw a church hall full of people. Then he went deaf and blind and he died too, and man, we just cried and cried.

—Oh my God, says Marje. —What a sad story. And Ron looks at her again like she is a lump of shit.

—But sometimes we laughed, you know. And sometimes we'd sing or tell stories or jokes.

Jokes, I think. I will ask him to tell me some of them later, I will. Maybe in bed. Ron is thinking the same thing because he is looking at me very intent, he knows how I love to hear a joke, he knows how that's one of the things I most like doing in bed, telling jokes and hearing them. And taking cocks in my mouth.

—Just stupid little things would make us laugh, says Izzi. —Like sharks chasing shoals of fish, or birds behaving stupid. Then Dutch, he found snails stuck to the bottom of the raft, and boy, we were so goddamn happy. One of the happiest days of my life, man. Imagine that. Imagine discovering you could eat live sea-snails being a happy moment!

I didn't have no war like Izzi's war, or any man's war, I thought. The war I had, it was my little war, a woman's war, a nobody's war. There were millions of us living that war, thousands of girls like me in Bristol, or like Marje or like Iris. We never had to float on no raft or eat sea-snails or watch Maddox go to the bottom of the sea with his hair, or get hit in the cockpit by shrapnel and make a tourniquet while we was holding the joystick. We queued for potatoes and we went to the flicks and we heard bombs fall so often it was background noise, you didn't even bother to stop what you were doing when the Moaning Minnies started up, you just go on with your business, even if you was bombed out again and again and again like Mrs Blathershite O'Malley. My war, it was a tiny little war compared to some. But mine stayed with me, and the things it made me do, they stayed with me too, but hidden.

Marje has gone to the Ladies' Room and Izzi has gone to order more drinks and Ron is still looking at me, his eyes haven't left me all evening. He is jealous, there is jealousy burning up in him, thinking of what me and Izzi are going to do together later.

—You're still a swell kid, he says.

—I haven't changed, I tell him. —I waited for you. I thought you'd come back.

—I know, hon, he says. —It all happened real fast. I crashed the plane coming home, see, I was gonna write you from the hospital –

—Stop, I murmur. Because in comes Marje, her eyes are red.

—I want to go home, she says to Ron. —Will you take me home, Ron? Now, please?

He sighs, narked.

—OK, Marje. How about you, Gloria? he goes.

—Oh I think I'll stay here and have another drink with Izzi, I tell him. —Swap a few jokes.

Because it gives me pleasure to make him jealous, make him picture my body tangled up with Izzi's on a motel bed.

—Sure, says Ron slowly, still looking at me all intense. —You have yourself a nice time, Gloria. You come home safe whenever you're ready. OK? You look after Gloria here for me, Izzi? Nice seeing ya, pal.

But his eyes, they hurt.

In the bar some more people come and join me and Izzi, and the conversation turns to a baseball team called the Yankees and the jukebox is playing and I'm all bubbles like I can be sometimes, telling jokes and funny stories and looking happy. But underneath I'm itching to see Ron again. Itching, aching, dying. Face all hot, heart all maimed still, the wound open and alive and only one way to heal it.

So when the bar closes Izzi offers me a lift back to Ron and Marje's place, and when we say goodbye he don't insist on nothing, just gives me a peck on the cheek, he is a good Italian boy what goes to church. Plus he never does come up with any decent jokes, they're all jokes I've already heard from Ron.

—It'd be nice to see you again some day, Gloria, he says. —I'm here another week.

I let myself in and wait downstairs in the dark of their living-room with no noise but the clock ticking on the wall. The kitchen door's open and a bit of light comes through to where I am, just enough to see by. I lie on the sofa, waiting.

He comes down into the kitchen at three o'clock, with no clothes on, just a towel round his waist. Sees me, goes to the ice-box and gets out a root beer.

—You have a nice evening with Izzi, Gloria?

—Yes thanks.

—He's a good guy.

—He brought me home.

I get up and go over to him, and watch as he takes a swig. In the silence I can hear him swallow and the beer going down his throat. The towel hides most of his scar, so you can just see the last couple of stitches. He swings round all of a sudden, angry.

—You make out in his car? (His voice is cracked.) —Did ya?

—Is that your business?

He looks at me, his eyes hurting again.

—I guess not, Gloria. Just curious. Sorry, hon.

There's a long silence and he swigs more beer, looking

at me. His chest, it's beautiful like it always was, and his tummy, it's still flat like geography.

—And did you fuck Marje when you came back? I whisper.

He looks away.

—Gloria. Don't.

—Why not? You should, she's your wife. You should fuck her every day.

He puts down the beer and moves towards me.

—Look at you, Gloria. (His hands on my hips, settled there where they belong.) —You're so beautiful. Jeez, I missed you, sweetheart.

—Did you?

—Sure I did. And you missed me. You think you can hide it?

His gravelly voice that used to make me melt, but now it's slurred from the beer. And then we're kissing, kissing and kissing – the longest kiss we ever had, that's full of wanting and violence. It starts there by the ice-box but before long it brings us to the floor, it is so strong, there is no resisting and no wanting to neither. And then we're down on the floor and he's tearing at my buttons and when he finds what he wants – the two of them (Aah, he goes, I missed these, honey, I so missed them) and he is in my arms again and I am in his and this is where we are meant to be.

And we have gone back in time to how it was before, before the war came along, and when he's in me – aah, where he belongs – the way he moves inside me brings the old happy loving times sweeping in, on and on it goes, the past all whooshing back, this is how it's meant to be, and I start crying because it's the most beautiful bloody thing that ever there was in the entire bloody world.

And then when it's over he pulls out and we lie there kissing on the floor. Don't even bother getting up. What for. Just stay there all night, doing it. Doing it again and again, making up for all that lost time.

—How could you do it to me?

—I don't know, hon. I don't know. She was there. She was unhappy.

—And now she's here. And still unhappy.

—Unhappy?

—You both are. Look at you. 'Marry in haste, repent at leisure' – you two could be a walking advertisement for it. You ballsed it up, Ron. And there's no going back. No wonder you get depressed and aggressive. It's not concussion that's to blame. It's Marje.

He's still a talker. But the things he talks about is sadder, like the best part of his life is gone for ever. He's grounded now, my airman. No more blue skies.

—Life sure is different now. Jeez, you come back here, you got no wings no more, man. You're back workin' in Pop's garage all day for jack shit, just one of them little ants again. Up there you was something else, you know, hon? Up there you had this vision, I'm tellin' ya. Down here you got no vision except what's right bang in front of ya. And that ain't so pretty, I tell ya.

—So why did you go off with Marje? I can't stop asking him this, I am like a dog at a bone, won't let it drop.

—I told ya. She was there, hon. She needed me real bad, after Bobby. We got kinda close. And – well. Man needs a woman, too.

—Doesn't need to marry her, when he's sposed to be marrying her sister.

He frowns.

—Was I?

And my heart sinks right down. What a bloody fool

you are, Gloria. He can't remember it, can he. He was too drunk.

It was just one of the things he said.

I am hungry, I am. So hollow, I could eat a horse.

—If we was in Chicago now we could go into one of them diners and order breakfast. Pancakes and maple syrup, I'd have, and some of them eggs over-easy. And American coffee instead of acorns and rats and Spam.

—Acorns and rats and Spam? she goes, all sleepy. —What are you on about, Gran?

—Here's a good one. Want to hear a good one?

—Go ahead.

—OK, there's Jesus, right. He's been crucified and he's dead. Anyway, three days later, Doubting Thomas is down by the Sea of Galilee fishing, and up walks Jesus and says, Hi there, Thomas. And Thomas says, But, Jesus, you're supposed to be dead! I came back to life, says Jesus. But Doubting Thomas don't like the sound of this, that's where the Doubting part of his name comes from, see. Prove it's you, he says. Prove to me that you're really Jesus rose from the dead and not an impostor. OK, says Jesus, what d'you want me to do? Well, the real Jesus used to do miracles, says Doubting Thomas. The real Jesus, he could walk on water. Righty-ho then, says Jesus, I will walk on water for you, just watch. And he hitches up his robes and he starts walking out on to the Sea of Galilee. Oh my God! goes Thomas. It is Jesus after all! But just then he notices that Jesus is getting a bit lower in the water – in fact he's starting to sink. Oh no! So Thomas dives in and swims out to Jesus, who's nearly drowning, and does his life-saving bit and hauls him back on to dry land. Oh Jesus, he says, I am so sorry I made you do that, I am so sorry I doubted you! That's OK, says Jesus. But tell me, says Thomas, how come you started to sink? Well, says Jesus. I didn't have these bloody holes in my feet last time, did I?

She likes that one she does, because she's laughing and waking up. Jokes, they're like the past, they are. They pop up out of the blue, you don't expect them. But jokes usually cheer you up and the past, you can't count on it to do that, can you.

Marje is getting twitchier every minute of course, as you'd guess, because after that night in the bar with Izzi and what happened after, we're barely bothering to hide it. Her getting a taste of her own medicine, I should coco. And of course one day we're at it – on their bed this time, no shame, us, no talking about it neither, it's all just biology between us now, and in she comes, back early from work.

Brave, I'll give her that. She watches for a long time. Seeing how it's done.

Must have been standing there at the door for ages before we notice her, her face is frozen, her mouth sagging down. Then she starts yelling stuff, and Ron leaps off me and grabs his pants and pulls them on sharpish. I don't do nothing though, do I, I just lie there starkers thinking: big deal, sis. It's only what you did to me, in London. Because she is pretty much dead to me by then, isn't she.

—Did you stay in touch? says the girl.

—She wrote me an evil letter. Then nothing for a few years. He wrote to me when she got cancer, but she didn't die from it. They'd had a couple of children by then. After that I got a card once a year, signed by both of them. I never replied. They were both dead, see. She said we'd always be sisters, but we weren't.

—So after she caught you and Ron – you left?

—Walked straight out there and then. Hitched a car ride with Izzi back to New York. We were through. Anyway, by then I'd got what I wanted, hadn't I.

—What did you want?

She is slow on the uptake, isn't she.

—I wanted what I got. I wanted the thing I came back with.

You can see her pale face now in the light, her little nose-stud glinting. She don't get it, does she.

—Marje was right. You've got to grab love. You've got to grab any kind of future that's got love in it. Even if it's just a little babby from a man who's no good.

Her nose-stud glinting in the half-light like a little tiny Christmas decoration. The moon outside, floating pale and alone.

GADDERTON LAKE

Christmas has died a death, I must've slept, there is no more turkey and that dirty old monkey used to sit in the chair over there has been cremated, he used to try it on with me, he once stuck his thing in my whatsit, I told Mrs M this and I told Hank and the Jill woman and I kept telling everyone at the funeral but no one wanted to know, not even the bloody vicar. What kind of listening ear is that then.

Today it is almost like spring, and it is a nice day. It is a nice day in springtime or in the month of May, so we have packed the car, two cars, one is Hank's, a Renault 19, the other is Jill's Mercedes, her slutty daughter is learning to drive so she has L-plates. This is an outing to Gadderton Lake that hasn't got no more ice on it now but it did before it was springtime or the month of May. Jill, she is wearing a nice smart coat that will get some mud on if she don't watch out. And did I mention her daughter Melanie, the one with the snake coming out of her bum that calls me Gran? She is here too, and Conchita la Paz, who is friends with her, and Calum who is talking now, saying poo and wee and no and also Granny once, so he is not such a bad little bastard, and has a yellow trike.

—What's green and goes up and down? I go.

—He's too young for jokes, Mum, says Hank. —He's only two!

—Two ain't too young. What's green and goes up and down, Calum? I told you jokes this young, I did. What's green and goes up and down?

I wait for him to say, Dunno, but he's busy with his trike.

—A gooseberry in a lift!

He don't laugh, probably ain't met a gooseberry yet, should've said kiwi fruit, never mind, try another.

—How did Captain Hook die?

—Tell me, says Jill.

—Scratched his arse with the wrong hand.

Jill looks away but me and Hank, we laugh and laugh, cos we love that one, we do. We never forget a joke.

It's a fresh-air day, the weather's warmish, and the sun shining like a plastic lid up there. In the Portakabin a lady's knitting a pink woolly for a baby, maybe she is a granny too.

The fishermen is parked there with their rods and placcy macs and little criss-cross stools, and the reeds shine glossy at you bright green, and the dead bulrushes is brown but a bright brown in the sun, it hurts your eyes. Hank's Wife buys ices from the knitting lady in the Portakabin. I have one called a Mr Big and so does Hank. Jill and Hank's Wife has made the picnic, Jill has done the savouries and Hank's Wife has done the sweet stuff, it is sandwiches and tortilla wraps and little pork pies and a sliced Battenberg. Calum spills the crisps under the picnic table and then a big magpie all comes pecking. One for sorrow.

—Nice coat, I tell the Jill woman. —Where d'you get it?

—Harrods, she says, and she and Hank's Wife look at each other.

—In a sale?

She smiles.

—Full price, I'm afraid. And I'm just opening my mouth to ask how much when she says – Four hundred and seventy-eight pounds.

Well, you could knock me down with a feather.

She's smiling like she's given me a present.

—D'you hear that, Hank? I yell at him. —Four hundred and seventy-eight squids! She's rolling in money, your new girlfriend!

And there's this look goes between him and her, and they both open their mouths to say something then think: oh never mind and shut them and smile instead. Lovers, eh. I was young once, I was a swell kid, I had a lover, his name was Ron but he said Raan.

—And my skirt cost eighty-three pounds, from John Lewis, she says, showing it me. And the shirt is from Peter Jones in London, it was around fifty pounds if I remember. And this necklace was a present from my husband before he died and I don't know how much it cost but it was probably over three hundred pounds.

—He got ripped off, I tell her.

But secretly I am gobsmacked, I am, because at last my daughter and I are having a conversation. Then another magpie comes along so it is all right, it is two for joy.

—Another joke for you, Hank? I yell across.

—Go on then, Mum.

We used to have joke sessions the two of us, we did. Back in Tooting. Used to laugh till we widdled.

—There was two men talking about women and one says to the other, I am a tit man myself. And the other one says, Tit man? Did you say tit man? That is very sexist. So the other one thinks for a minute and he says, OK, sorry. Tit person.

That's a funny one, that is. Even Jill, she smiles.

The Melanie girl and Conchita la Paz is off giggling somewhere, having a look to see what the other fisher-men've caught, and seeing who's worth flirting with because they is teenagers. And Jill is playing with Calum and Hank is casting his rod and going Shhh, everyone, but he don't give a hoot if he catches one or not, I know my Hank, he just likes being by the water, if he don't catch a Hallelujah fish he ain't never bothered.

—This is a lovely picnic you've done for us, Karen, I tell Hank's Wife. You have done us proud, you have.

And then for some reason she bursts into tears. Talk about moody.

—You called me Karen, she goes.

—Well, it's your name, isn't it? As far as I'm aware?

—Yes, Gloria, she says, blowing a big blow into a napkin. —It's my name.

All right. So that is that cleared up then.

I have lived a life, I have. I have been places and done stuff and seen lots about the world on telly and I have lived through the war. I did my bit for my country with my Victory onions and working in munitions and keeping hens, I ain't no war criminal, I was just a girl made mistakes, stupid-girl mistakes thinking that carpets are for sweeping stuff under when my mum could've told me any day, No, that is not the case, my girl, it is not the case for you and it is not the case for no one, the dirt comes out somehow or other, no matter what, the first crime is the first crime but pretend it ain't done and you are doing a second crime and then maybe there will be a third and no one will learn nothing.

That what my mum would've said or anyone with a grain of sense but I was the stupid one, remember.

Anyway look at me, it weren't a bad life even if it got a bit snafued. I have raised a good son and done him proud, taken him to Blackpool on holiday, he can't complain about me being a bad mum, I was the best bloody mother there ever was to that boy. So this'll do me here, in the sunshine, with some people about who seems to know me. There is a tiny pilot light wants to switch itself off now. It is like shutting out a little light, a little trembling pilot light in your head.

Easier than you think, you know.

You'll see.

And when the light has gone out, there is just a little glow left behind, where you were. Look at you there in the wheelchair, so old, so old you look, Gloria, how did you go on so long. You were a swell kid once, you were a real A-one honey. And nobody has seen yet what has happened, and that is all right, because afterwards they will say what a peaceful way to go, sitting by the lake, looking out at the water.

All right, this is.

In the green water which is green I can see the little girl floating but upright, and Doris who is waving. There they are, and there's Zedorro, and the Slut Fairy, and Ron, and Marje, and my mum and dad, and Bobby and Mrs Blathershite O'Malley and Iris who is whole again, and the Jew woman who got the guilt squirming in me, there she is with the others, on the water's skin, shining where it's clear above the mud. Not staring full of hate no more, cos her face it has gone gentle at last, and I would like my face to go gentle like that.

Would I care to join them, they are wondering. Would I care to join them on Gadderton Lake. Floating on the green water.

On the green clear water of Gadderton, where the past and the future and the now-time is all one, and if you open your mouth the taste of the water tells you, Yes, yes, yes, Gloria, you are forgiven.

And I am.

Acknowledgements

I am indebted to *The New Yorker Book of War Pieces*, for background material about GIs during World War Two. Occasionally I have quoted directly from soldiers' personal accounts of their war experiences, but mostly I have modified and re-invented their accounts to fit my story. Particularly inspiring were A.J. Liebling's 'The Foamy Fields', Hank Murphy's 'Eighty-Three Days', and Brendan Gill's 'Young Man Behind Plexiglas'. Also very helpful were *Diary of a Bristol Woman 1938–45* by V.A.M., and *Sentimental Journey, the Story of the GI Brides* by Pamela Winfield – who was kind enough to read my manuscript, and correct a multiplicity of factual errors.

I am grateful to the Society of Authors, who provided a travel grant which enabled me to visit 'GI bride' Olivia Poole and her husband John, of Corona del Mar, California. Fortunately for the Pooles, they are as unlike Gloria and Ron as it is possible to be. But they generously shared with me their many vivid memories of wartime Britain, and life back in America after the war. I am eternally grateful for this, and for their friendship.

A Note on the Author

Liz Jensen is the acclaimed author of *The Paper Eater*, *Egg Dancing* and *Ark Baby*, which was shortlisted for the *Guardian* Fiction Prize. She lives in London.

A NOTE ON THE TYPE

The text of this book is set in Linotype Sabon, named after the type founder, Jacques Sabon. It was designed by Jan Tschichold and jointly developed by Linotype, Monotype and Stempel, in response to a need for a typeface to be available in identical form for mechanical hot metal composition and hand composition using foundry type.

Tschichold based his design for Sabon roman on a fount engraved by Garamond, and Sabon italic on a fount by Granjon. It was first used in 1966 and has proved an enduring modern classic.